FRANKIE'S STORY

'You all right, Frankie?' Gerry asked, anxiously.

I felt like saying sure I was. My Dad had run off, my house had gone mad, and the wee boys were painting things about me on shed doors, the sort of things that might lead to a knee-cap job.

'I'm just fine and dandy,' I said.

CATHERINE SEFTON

FRANKIE'S STORY

MAMMOTH

First published in Great Britain 1988
by Hamish Hamilton Children's Books
Methuen Teens paperback edition first published 1989
Published 1990 by Teens Mandarin
Reissued 1995 by Mammoth
an imprint of Reed Consumer Books Limited
Michelin House, 81 Fulham Road, London SW3 6RB
and Auckland, Melbourne, Singapore and Toronto

Copyright © 1988 Catherine Sefton

ISBN 0 7497 0558 2

A CIP catalogue record for this title
is available from the British Library

Printed and bound in Great Britain
by Cox & Wyman Ltd, Reading, Berkshire

For Helen and Warren

Notice to all Readers

Chapter 1

'Frankie! Frankie!' Geraldine shouted. 'Look out the window. Cops!'

I belted across and joined her, flopping down on the bed on top of her books. She is supposed to be studying for her mocks, but she isn't. I'm in no position to criticise, after my performance.

We both peered out through the blinds, keeping our heads low, so that they wouldn't spot us.

'It's like Dodge City round here!' Gerry said, with some satisfaction. Well, it was a bit of excitement. Not that we needed excitement, with the way things have been going in our house.

There were four R.U.C. men ... that's Royal Ulster Constabulary, our cops ... and another one in the car attending to the radio, so they had come mob-handed, all dolled up in their flak jackets. They were outside the Hagens' house. It would be Hagens'! They have had more visitations from the R.U.C. than anyone else on the Estate, and that is saying something, given that our Estate is a fair way down the road to proclaiming itself a Catholic Republic all on its oney-o.

My Mother came into the room, all floppy slippers and alarm.

'Geraldine! Frankie!' she said. 'Come away out of that!'

'No way!' I said. 'The cops are rounding up the Hagens!'

'The Daddy probably battered somebody's head in,' said Gerry cheerfully.

'I bet the wee Hagens set fire to the school again,' I said.

'Or wrote "Up the Provos" on the wall,' said Gerry.

The end gable of the row the Hagens live in is covered in Republican slogans and painted flags. It is their way of showing the world, but it doesn't go down well with most of the neighbours, considering the gable isn't attached to the Hagens' house. The Provo supporters don't mind, I suppose, and the others can't do much about it, for fear of getting a stone through the window. Anyway, the words are on the wall, and as far as the cops are concerned that makes everybody down here a potential cop-killer, which we're not. I never killed anybody, but I wouldn't risk my neck taking the writing *off* the wall, and neither would anyone else.

'Whatever is going on, it is no cause for entertainment!' Mum said, but she didn't drag us away from the window. We're too big to drag, and I suppose she wanted to know what was happening, like anybody else would.

I decided that that was it, and so I laid on a commentary.

'Mrs Hagen is at the upstairs window in her pink and blue nightie and she is shouting at Sergeant Moran and she's real mad,' I said.

'That woman!' Mum said, shaking her head.

'Wait a bit,' I said. 'One of the R.U.C. men has gone up to the door and ... Oh!'

'Oh what?' said Mum, paddling over to us.

The cop had broken the glass at the side of the Hagens' front door. He reached in and undid the door catch, and they all charged into the house.

They must have met Mrs Hagen and her back-yard brush charging *out*, for the next thing we saw was a bottle green R.U.C. hat flying through the air, and rolling in the snow, and after it came two R.U.C. men and Mrs Hagen, complete with yard-brush and nightie, all in a staggery ball that foundered on Brendan Hagen's rusty trike. They went down in the snow, with Mrs Hagen belting at the cops with her brush and them trying to keep a grip on her. She was giving as good as she got, and better, part with the brush and part with the lip, and her language wasn't ordinary.

The Belly Kelly from next door came to his window, but he didn't come out. Old Belly stood there in his braces, leaning on an old hurley stick, watching the fight. The Belly was one of the original Civil Rightsers, who got his head beaten in by the cops for his trouble. He doesn't *like* the cops, but he has no time for cowboys like the Hagens, either.

The next move came from Danny Hagen. Danny is Mrs Hagen's middling son, the joy-rider. The eldest is Patrick, who is doing one of the Government schemes as cheap labour on the bin lorries, and then there is Eamonn who is in a Home, and Maureen and Roisin and the last of all is wee Brendan, the Daddy Hagen's afterthought. Everybody says that the Daddy should have a vasectomy.

It was Danny the joy-rider who came flying out over the back wall at the end of the row, in his pyjama bottoms, and belted up the pavement towards our house.

The Hagens live at number 7, Unity Park. We are up the dead end, Unity Close. Danny came running by us, holding his pyjamas up because he'd lost the buttons, and an R.U.C. man came flopping over the wall and headed after him. Meanwhile Mrs Hagen and *her* cops were still rolling around the garden. Sergeant Moran came out of the house and looked at them. Then he spotted Danny and set off to join the wall-dropping cop in hot pursuit.

'Isn't it great!' Geraldine said, all excited.

'It's a disgrace!' my Mum said.

'Aye, but it is great just the same!' Geraldine said.

Danny doubled down the entry by Maguire's house ... that is number 23 ... with Sergeant Moran and the young cop bellowing and bawling and slipping and sliding after him in their big boots. Danny was in his bare feet, which must have been frozen, but still allowed him to keep upright whilst he ran.

'Back window!' I shouted, and I beat Gerry across the landing to it.

Our back looks out on the weed patch we call a garden, and then there is *our* fence, and a big ditch, and then the barbed wire fence round the Caravan park, where the tourists come in summer. It is like a Concentration Camp without the look-out towers, a great big fortification to keep the locals out, or the tourists in, I'm not sure which. Maxie McCall runs it, and he calls it EL SILVER DOLLAR RANCHO only he won't spend any of his silver dollars on the drains, which make a big stink and a fly heaven in the summer. If we all die of the plague, we'll come back and haunt Maxie.

Danny got over the fence at the back of our row, and down into the big ditch, but that is about as far as he got, because he disappeared up to the top of his pyjama trousers in the snow that was lying in it. He floundered about, trying to get himself up the back and hang himself on the barbed wire, with the young cop standing on the bank above, laughing at him.

By this time the half of Unity Close that backs onto the Silver Dollar had a face at every window, some of them egging Danny on and some of them shouting at Sergeant

Moran and the cop. In the background we could hear the wails of Mrs Hagen from her garden, giving out like a banshee. She had been deprived of her brush, which had been arrested.

Then someone started bin lid banging. It must have been the Curlys, or the Hartys, three doors up from us, but it set the cops in action again, mindful that someone might decide they were a good target for a bullet if they hung about too long.

My Mum heard the bins going.

'Come away from that window this minute!' she said, from the bathroom doorway. 'Two big girls like you! You should be ashamed of yourselves.'

'Okay, Mum,' I said. 'Keep your hair on!' And I came away, but I nipped downstairs to the front room, and had a look through the venetians at the cops loading Danny and Mrs Hagen and her brush into their car. Micky Harty came out of his house and ran down the pavement after the cops, and Teresa Harty, his sister, was out in her housecoat shrieking her head off, as if she'd been raped.

'Would you listen to that one!' Gerry said.

'She was just the same in school,' I told her. We used to go to the Cross and Passion Primary with Teresa Harty. Teresa punched a wee girl one time and broke her teeth. She said it was because the wee girl had nits.

The whole rent-a-crowd lot turned out, too late, for the cops had gone, but instead they wound up comforting Teresa, though what they were comforting Teresa for I couldn't figure. It isn't as if Danny Hagen was her boy-friend, or something. She's got her eye on Con McCluskey, but Con's a sight too smart to get himself mixed up with the Hartys ... he'd use them all right, but that is as far as it goes. Con's the big man around here, and everybody knows it.

'I honestly don't know about the Hagens,' Mum said, shaking her head. She had come downstairs after me. 'Those poor kids! What a way to bring them up.'

'The Daddy is a head case,' I said. 'And the rest of the family takes after him!'

'At least they have stuck together,' Geraldine said, from the doorway.

Mum went stiff, her own peculiar way, like stiff jelly.

'Well, they have, haven't they?' Gerry said.

'Yes,' Mum said.

She turned round and looked at Geraldine, and then she went into the kitchen, slamming the door behind her so that the partition rocked and almost deposited our photos on the floor. It is that sort of house. You slam a door somewhere, and the world knows about it.

'There was absolutely no call for that!' I said.

'Wasn't there?' Gerry said.

'That was mean, and you know it!' I said.

'I don't care,' Gerry said, 'It isn't my fault, is it? I didn't get us into this mess.'

'Who do you think did then?' I said.

Geraldine nodded at the kitchen door.

'*And* Dad,' I said. 'Not just her. You can't blame it all on her, you know.'

'I know whose side I'm on,' Gerry said.

'You don't have to be on anybody's side,' I said. 'It isn't like that.'

'Always has been up to now!' Gerry said, and she swiped her coat off the back of a chair, and slung it on. Then she wound her stripey green and purple scarf around her neck, and put on her mittens.

6

I let her do it.

I wasn't going to give her the satisfaction of arguing with her. She was the one who always made a song and dance about being Daddy's Little Girl, and she hasn't got it sorted out yet. She's only fifteen. She has no sense.

She takes the Dad thing personally, but it was a disaster for all of us.

I love him too.

'Tell me I'll understand better when I'm grown up!' she said, and she headed for the front door, though where she thought she was going at ten past nine in the morning in Unity Close is beyond me. 'Anyway, you're a fine one to talk after the way you have been carrying on,' was her parting shot.

I straightened the pictures on the wall. Photos. Us at school. Mum. Mum's Mum. The signed one of the Pope No Dad. I don't know what she did with his photo, or the wedding group. Probably chucked them in the bin. If she had chucked them in the bin, it was the wrong thing to do. I could see why she'd do it, but I wished she hadn't. She was trying to wipe him out, as if he had never been in our lives. Well, it isn't so. My Dad *was* in my life, and he still is. Because I can't forget how it used to be, and I don't want to, because my Dad was the biggest thing there was in my life, till the rows started with my Mum. My mistake was siding with her because I was sorry for her, and because it wasn't fair that Gerry and I were on his side, and she was on her own. I took sides, and sort of cut him off from me ... and then the next time I looked round, he was gone ... and maybe it was my fault.

I have this trick of thinking that everything that happens, happens because of me, and it doesn't work that way ... other people have their own lives, and they live them, and there are always going to be bits of their lives that are apart from the people you would think be closest to them.

Mum still hadn't come out of the kitchen.

It was probably have-a-weep time, and I had no stomach for it. I went off upstairs, taking my time, and I put my housecoat on. Then I came down again to face the fireworks.

'Hi you!' I said.

'Hi you!' Mum said, with a sniff. It's a game between us, that. It has been since I don't know when. She was all red and puffy faced again, over by the sink, letting on that she was all right.

'She's away out,' I said. 'Our Geraldine.'

'Yes,' Mum said.

'Maybe the fresh air will blow some wit into her,' I said.

'I doubt it,' Mum said.

She stood at the sink with her back to me. I was scoring zero in communication.

'It is dead cold,' I said, trying to get things back on a level I could cope with. I wasn't kidding! It *was* dead cold. It comes of the storage heaters. They are supposed to heat the whole Unity Park Estate, but nobody here turns them on, because nobody can afford to run them. We have to make do with Calor gas burners or electric fires. We don't have real gas fires, because there are no gas mains. The Calor gas ones are great for the Silver Dollar caravans, but they don't work too well in the house, and everything gets soaked and mouldy with condensation. The man who built Unity Park Estate may have had a great team of social engineers behind him, building community bridges, but he did what he did with old cheap plaster and breezeblock, and took his designs from a Bargain Book, because there isn't a decent house in the place. It's the same on the other Estate, Sandhills, where all the Protestants moved to, when

8

the Catholics moved over to Unity Park. All the houses are rotten from the plaster to the door frames, that's what my Dad says.

It is what he used to say, before he went off on us.

He doesn't say it any more, because he isn't here.

Nobody knows where he is, except possibly Geraldine, and I can't ask her, because she wouldn't tell me anyway. We've gone our different ways, me and Geraldine.

'Oh, cheer up, Mum,' I said, feeling really fed up with her, because I can't cope with a glum Mum, and I shouldn't have to.

Sometimes I think the only enjoyment Mum gets these days is having her scenes ... she manages about two a day, and most of them have the same words in, only she varies the intensity. And when she isn't having scenes, Gerry is, which leaves me piggy-in-the-middle. They're just like each other, those two, my Mum and Gerry.

I suppose that leaves me like my Dad.

'It's being compared to the Hagens that gets me,' Mum said, twisting at her wedding ring ... the wedding ring twists are always a bad sign. 'Whatever else about us, we were never as bad as that.'

'Nobody says you were,' I said.

'But they're still together,' she said. 'The Daddy Hagen and his prize fighter lady, rolling around the pubs, and a houseful of little Hagens, each with a record as long as your arm.'

'So?' I said.

'So I'd like to know where I went wrong,' she said, and I thought: *and I'd like to know why it is me that has to stand here and listen to it* but I didn't say it, because I knew the answer.

It was all down to my Dad.

Chapter 2

Philip Moore came round for me about four, as we'd arranged, and we went down the town. We weren't going anywhere, just out. I don't go to Philip's house, because Mrs Moore doesn't like me. That's partially because I'm a Catholic, although she's too civilised to say that to Philip, and partially because she thinks everyone on Estates has fleas ... *both* Estates that is, she reckons fleas are ecumenical.

Patrick Hagen was out at the front of Hagens' house as we went by, fixing a bit of hardboard on the broken door. He gave us a wave.

'Hi, Paddy!' Philip said.

'Phil. Frankie,' Patrick said.

'Hi, Patrick,' I said.

It wasn't what you could call an illuminating conversation. Patrick probably wasn't in the mood for one, and Philip was uneasy. Philip always *is* uneasy, coming slumming in the ghetto. He doesn't know many down our way, except me. That is, he knows them, in the way he knew Patrick, because Ballybeg is too *small* not to know people, but he doesn't know them really. He knows them the way they know him. And the Hagens he would know more about than most, I suppose, on account of the way the Hagens keep getting themselves arrested.

'Is it bin day round here?' Philip said, reading my

10

thoughts. What he was getting at was *why isn't Patrick Hagen on his bin lorry*? I didn't put him out of his misery, because I didn't want to start the whole story of the Hagens' visitation from the cops. These things are bad enough to live with, without going round boasting about them.

Time was when I would have told Philip, straight off. That was when we were all Romeo and Juliet—Young Love conquering all ... only it *wasn't*. I was thinking *what am I doing with him anyway*, and the only thing I could come up with was that I was doing it out of devilment, asking for trouble. I'd got a bad name for going out with the Wrong Sort, and the likes of the Hartys had me on their list. Dumping-the-Protestant-boyfriend would be like giving in to them, but it didn't seem like all that good a reason for *not* dumping Phil, either.

So I thought: *I'm going to make up my mind about this*. but I didn't say that to Philip. I just said: 'I feel sorry for Patrick Hagen sometimes.'

'Oh yeah?' said Phil, primly.

'Imagine having that lot for a family,' I said.

'I'd rather not, thank you very much,' Phil said, picking up his pace. He's thin and beaky, and his old nose was blue with the cold. He had a drip coming. He took out his hanky and blew his nose. It was like a fog horn. You would think Mrs Moore would have taught him to blow his nose properly when he was a wee Protestant in the pram.

It is about three quarters of a mile in from Unity Park to the town, a right hoof. They stuck the Estates out on two adjoining roads with no shops and no buses barring the one-every-two-hours-if-it-comes Fortwilliam bus, so that they could keep the riff-raff out of the way. They reckoned we could stay out there and throw stones at each other rightly, without breaking any of the shop windows. That's what I think, anyway.

We trudged on past the garage somebody closed down with a petrol bomb, and the boarded-up front of the chipboard factory that isn't any more, where my Dad used to be shop steward before he got laid off and told he was useless like everybody else round here. Ballybeg College of Further Education, otherwise known as the Tech, has it for Industrial Training now, but it was all shut up because it was out of term.

PROVOS RULE! said the big white letters on the wall round the factory, and BRITS OUT and SS R.U.C. BASTARDS and TIOCFAIDH ÁR LÁ—*Our Day Will Come* and BRENDAN RODGERS IS A ... Whatever Brendan Rodgers was they had scrubbed it out, or he had scrubbed it out. Then there was another message:

WE GOT BOB ALLEN

Bob Allen was a Catholic, a retired policeman. He was in the Chess Club with my Dad. They were very friendly. He was a decent man. The Provos shot him over his garden wall, right through the spine. Now he can't walk. He just sits there in a special chair, and people come and walk him about, but not very far. He's afraid to go out, in case they come to finish the job.

My Dad went mad about it.

If Belly Kelly hadn't stopped him, Dad would have gone round to McCluskeys' and given Con McCluskey an earful. But the Belly was right. Somebody like my Dad shouting in the front garden wouldn't change anything, not as far as Con is concerned. The cops knew fine well who was behind it, but they couldn't do a thing. They never even lifted Con, or tried to plant stuff on him, or anything. It would have been a no-hoper. The day Bob Allen got done Con will have been well out of it, with a stack of witnesses to say so. That's the way it works. Con didn't pull the trigger, but he put the bullet in Bob Allen just the same, and that's why Bob Allen is where he is, in a wheelchair, and Con is where he is, sitting pretty, out on the Estate, where he's a kind of cross between God and Gerry Adams. Bob Allen was another mark against us, for Mrs Moore, and Philip for that matter, though he never said a thing, but I know he thought it. I don't see why me or my Dad or the likes of Belly Kelly should be tarred with the same brush as Con McCluskey, but we *are*, just because we live on the same Estate, and we're the same religion ... if you can call somebody like Con a Catholic, which you can't, not truly ... but *truly* if anybody did put a bullet in Con, which they won't, because the big guys never get it ... *if* they did, he'd be buried out of *our* church, with all the trimmings, the tricolour and the beret and gloves on his box.

I just hate it all for happening.

Phil blew his nose again. *Honk-honk!*

I tried to look as if I wasn't with him.

We came over the scrubland at the end of the road, and up Church Lane towards the Tech.

Skyscraper Calvert was at the gate. He said 'Hullo' and we said 'Hullo' back.

Skyscraper stamped his feet in the slush, and looked down at his big lace-up boots, inviting us to look too. He wears them to make everyone think he has a motorbike. He has the weirdest skinny legs, like a Daddy Longlegs. He must be about 6'6". Leaning against the Tech notice board beneath the AIDS ad is about all he can manage by

13

way of activity, even on a good day. On a bad day, I think he just stays in bed. He is supposed to be in the same Business Studies group as me, but he never makes it in. Maybe he's hoping for a job propping up the clouds.

Honk! went Phil.

I was beginning to get desperate!

'What are we going down the town *for*, Philip?' I asked him, hoping he'd surprise me. 'When you've finished blowing your nose, that is!'

'I don't know,' Phil said. His eyes were beginning to water, and he had laced his hanky through his fingers.

'When is something going to happen?'

'Some time, never,' Phil said, easing to a saunter now that he was clear of the ghetto quarter.

We went past the bank. That is where my Education might have got me, if I'd wanted it to, that or one of the shops on the Main Street. There *is* only one street, really, so the options aren't enormous. Maybe being the School Flop Out and an Awful Example for the Nuns to hold up to everyone wasn't so bad, after all!

'We should make something happen!' I said, as we turned off the Sea Road, onto the Prom. It was bleak. Ballybeg is a long flat place, strung out along the foot of the mountain, with a dingy clock tower in the middle, and a dingy station where dingy trains come half a dozen times in the day, on a side-track from the mainline.

Side-tracked, that's what we are.

'Who should?' Phil said, wiping his eyes.

'*You* should!' I said. 'I'm thick. I'm let off taking any initiative. You are supposed to be the genius.'

Doing A Levels and getting to the Ulster Polytech in Jordanstown doesn't make you a genius, I just said that to please him, but maybe he thought I had it about right.

14

All he said was: 'You are not *that* thick, Frankie!' meaning I *was* thick, but not as thick as I thought I was!

Big deal! I could feel myself going off him by the minute.

We came to a stop at the first shelter on the promenade. It is a little yellow wooden one, the centre of some frozen lives for most of the winter, to judge by the beer cans around it and the writing on the walls, which is strictly unrepeatable!

I picked up one of the beer cans, and chucked it at a frost bitten flower bed.

'You're a litter lout, Frankie,' Philip said.

The trouble was, he half meant it! He was looking around to see if his Mammy or his Grannie or the Presbyterian Minister had seen him, marooned with this weird-looking redhead Catholic from the Estate, who was chucking beer cans about. The weird-looking bit was my own fault, part of my mini revolution against life, and my sister Geraldine. They say there's always a frumpy one and a gorgeous one, and I'd picked my part; long red hair and my disaster coat with the C.N.D. badges on, and the suede collar turned up so I could bite it if life got too much.

'Any more of this old place, and I'm going on the glue!' I said.

Silence fell. Phil started sniffing, instead of honking. I think he sensed I was *off* the honks. Then, bang on cue, it started to snow.

The snow was blowing down off the mountain, wraithing across the prom. We sat on the side of the shelter that faced away from it, and watched the white webs form on the trees and lamp poles, where they string up the fairy lights in the summer.

Waiting for something to happen. *Anything*.

Phil gave a preparatory sniff, to clear the drip, and then

he sort of edged towards me, and something snapped.

'Oh, do give over!' I said, disgustedly.

He looked hurt.

He took out his hanky and unwound it, then he blew his nose.

Honk! Honk! went the hanky.

I didn't want to be Heathcliffed, not exactly, because that wouldn't go with the new free-me, but I couldn't live with the idea of being edged at by a *honk*!

'Can't we do something, Philip?' I said, desperately.

He thought a bit, trying not to look too rejected, and then he came up with a bright one.

'We could go back up the town to your place?' he suggested.

I got up.

'You sit there,' I said, when he began to rise. 'You just sit there till the snow forms over you. I'm off!'

I started down the Prom.

'Frankie?' he called from the shelter, sticking the lonely honker out in the air, where it could catch the snow.

'Don't hold your breath waiting for me to come back, Moore!' I said. 'I'm gone, gone, gone!'

He did what he was told, like a good little student.

A Total Creep.

I thought he might follow me up the road, so I hid in the Post Office, and by that time guilt was stirring.

You shouldn't be awful to anybody, not like that, especially someone soft inside like Phil, half decent even if he was a fool, and the Guardian of Tender Moments from Times Past, when we had shared the back seat in the bus, but just the same ...

'Frankie, dear?' It was Mrs Walsh, from the Harbour, not exactly the person I most wanted to see.

16

I mean, I *respect* her. She's a good person. She's the only one who really tried to help us, coping with my Mum, and Gerry's histrionics ... but that's the trouble. She got the whole bagful, from Mum and Gerry, and she must have been awful fed up with them. It made me awkward just to think of the amount of emotion they'd dumped on her, when she only got into it by accident, through her Jenny being Geraldine's friend. She didn't know us at all, really, and then suddenly she was right bang in the middle of a family drama, with Gerry shouting and Mum weeping on her shoulder and me ... well, it went on and on, and she did help, and I was really grateful, *but*. ...

'How are you, dear?' she said, tightening her grip on her handbag, like somebody in an aeroplane settling down for a bumpy ride.

'I'm fine,' I said.

'Your poor mother?' she said.

'She's fine too,' I said, lying in my teeth.

'And things have settled down a bit, by now?' she asked, hopefully.

'Yes,' I said.

I could have told her: *'No. My Mum is still all twisted up. Gerry is play-acting for all she is worth and I'm fed up,'* but I didn't.

She was cleverer than I thought she was!

'You're not telling me the truth, Frankie,' she said.

I was dead embarrassed. She'd caught me and I wasn't expecting it. She might be a wee lady in a sheepskin coat, with the handbag, but she wasn't going to let me away with my discreet evasions.

'No, I'm not,' I said.

'Well, at least that is honest,' she said.

She looked all natty and businesslike, but she drinks like

17

a fish. That is what Gerry says, and she ought to know. She is up at Mrs Walsh's house often enough, anyway.

'You're a daft wee girl,' she said. 'You mustn't let this trouble with your father ruin you.'

I felt like telling her it was no class of a conversation to be having in a Post Office.

'I know that, Mrs Walsh,' I said, and then I let go! 'I just don't want to talk to you about it. Is that all right?'

She *deserved* it! She had it coming for trying to interfere.

'Of course, it is a matter for yourself,' she said, and she went off and left me, with her lips zipped up like a purse. Help! Another one I'd offended.

I'm sick and tired of people telling me what I ought to do. I was sick with myself too for letting her see how upset I was ... *am*. I just couldn't put up with people patronising me, everybody going round saying Frankie-blew-it, she's a mess, because of her Dad.

I'm open to it, I suppose, because of the carry on at school. There they were, my Mum and everybody, and the nuns, all expecting I'd sail through despite my Dad clearing off, and there I was ... I just didn't want to do it.

So I didn't.

I ducked out on them.

Sister Attracta went mad! You'd have thought I'd turned Protestant or something. I was supposed to be smart ... we both are, me and Gerry ... and the old G.C.S.E. should have been a doddle ... but then everything blew up, and we were those girls-whose-Dad-ran-off-with-the-lady-behind-the-cheese-counter and I just felt I'd be that then, not a smart getting-exams-person, and my Mum and Dad and everyone who went round expecting me to be brave could take a running jump.

Of course, it backfired on me.

That's how I wound up doing Business Studies, instead of having my Big Career like Phil Moore.

All washed up ... washed up like a dead fish on the beach.

Everybody mad at me.

It was the only way I could get back at them ... at my Dad, really, I suppose. He was the one that used to talk to me, and read me things, and help me with my stuff when he could ... when Gerry wasn't swanning round him.

My Dad was the one who gave me the Big Ideas about degrees and courses and things, and then, just when it came to the bit ... he ran off with the cheese lady.

My school walk-out was my one big scene, but when the dust settled the other rows were still on the go. My Mum was still doing her act, and fighting the bit out with Gerry, and my Dad was still gone. The pair of them, my Mum and Gerry ... shouting round the house about *their* feelings, and how *they'd* been let down. I didn't shout *in* the house, but I made up for it out of the house, with nuns and teachers and strangers who wanted to interfere.

I got let down too.

In the end I was left with nobody to have a scene with! They'd all been scared off.

Chapter 3

I may have thought that that was the Montague-Capulet bit put firmly back into Shakespeare and out of my life, but it wasn't.

'News at Ten' time, and I was looking to see if there was something lively to turn over to ... and there wasn't, there never is when you need it, and I needed it after that nothing day ... when there was a ring at the door.

My Mum went.

I'm dead glad that I didn't.

There was a muttered conversation in the hall, I couldn't catch what was said, and then my Mum put her head round the living-room door.

'Frankie, do you happen to know where Philip Moore might be?'

'No,' I said.

'No idea?'

I shrugged.

My Mum closed the door behind, signing to me to stay put by shaking her head and pursing her lips. I had the distinct impression that she was about to enjoy herself.

I nipped over to the window, and peeked through the blinds. The Moores' Rover 3000 was parked outside, with Darky Moore, that's Phil's dad, at the wheel. Mrs Moore hurried down the pavement to it, and got in, slamming the door.

They drove off.

I went out to the hall.

My Mum was turning away from the Holy water after giving herself a good sprinkle, to cast off the evil spirits. There was a flush of satisfaction in her cheek, and it wasn't the cold. 'That is one unpleasant wee woman!' my Mum said. 'She as good as suggested that I was lying to her.'

'What's up?' I said.

What was up was that Phil hadn't showed up at home, after telling them he was only going out for an hour or two, to meet some friends. That must have been when he was coming down to our place, although he wouldn't have told his Mum that ... she was clever enough to guess it anyway. Apparently some of Darky Moore's solicitor friends came down from Belfast and Mrs Moore was mad at Philip for not being there. Then, when the friends had cleared off early because of the bad roads and the snow, she began to get worked up about where her Star Student son was, and in the end nothing would suit her but she would come round to our place and tear him out of my arms, which she strongly suspected he was in. Of course, *he wasn't*, and that is what my Mum told her, implying *he should be so lucky* and she says Mrs M. went on as if we were hiding Philip under the bed to hand over to the Jesuits, or something.

'She's a bigot,' I said. 'And snobbish with it!'

'Darky drinks too much,' Mum said. 'She's got nothing to be snobby about.'

Darky owns his own firm now in the city. Being a solicitor in Belfast these days is like winning the Pools. He has it made, getting all the para-militaries off, but Mrs Moore doesn't like being reminded where the money

21

comes from.

'I hope your Phil doesn't take after his father, that's all,' said Mum.

'He's not *my* Phil,' I said.

'Oh?' she said. 'That's a new tune.'

'Well, that's the way it is,' I said. I wasn't going to give her a blow by blow version of me and Phil on the Prom, with Phil getting his marching orders, because that was my business, but at the same time I wanted to get the message straight in her head. No more Philip Moore, the mixed marriage was off ... not that a *marriage* had ever been on ... and I was back in the Eligible-for-Marriage-to-a-Good-Catholic-Doctor-Stakes, which is the height of most people's ambitions round here.

Then Geraldine walked in.

'Where have you been all day?' Mum asked, rounding on her. It was a useful diversion. These days when my Mum gets her teeth into something she worries at it ... she doesn't *do* anything, but it goes on her brooding list for the long hours in the armchair watching Brookside and Emmerdale Farm, with no Dad to talk to. Her old programmes used to drive him mad anyway. He used to take his crossword book and sit in the kitchen when she switched on.

'Out,' Geraldine said.

'And where is "Out" when it is at home?' Mum said, putting on her martyred face, which is always a bad sign.

'Jenny Walsh's house,' Gerry said.

'You could have told me you were going up there,' Mum said, fastening onto the vibrations at once. After our Big Scene at the Walshs' house, with Mum and Gerry yelling at each other and little Mrs Walsh darting round

22

trying to soothe the pair of them, my Mum woke up to what a performance she'd made of it all. I think she avoids Mrs Walsh now, because she's embarrassed. So she should be! Mrs Walsh is a witness *against* her, and she doesn't like me or Gerry going there ... not that I do go, because I'm embarrassed myself about all the things Mrs Walsh knows about us ... things Gerry should never have told her, but she did. Personal things, that no stranger should have been in on ... a whole running commentary on The Marriage Breakdown, and Geraldine the Abandoned Child, and How Could Dad Do It To Her.

'I couldn't tell you, because I didn't know, did I?' said Gerry. 'I met Jenny Walsh, and went up with her, and Mrs Walsh made me some tea and then we had a natter ... I didn't mean to be this late back, that's all.'

'It seems the town is full of stray folk,' I said, getting in quickly before Mum would start a senate hearing about the conversation in Walshs'. The bottom line was that Gerry was testing Mum again, and the message behind it was, You've-no-authority-over-me-when-you-can't-even-keep-your-own-life-together.

'I'd rather you didn't go to Walshs' so often, Gerry,' my Mum said.

Gerry just ignored her.

I started gabbling about Mrs Moore, and what a nerve she had slagging Mum off at the door ... it was anything to change the conversation.

'I saw Phil!' Gerry said.

'Where?'

'Just ... just down the street,' Gerry said, glancing at Mum.

Mum caught it.

'*Where* down the street?' she said.

'Going that-a-way,' Gerry said, vaguely gesturing.

I waited till Mum was out of the way, then I rounded on her.

'Okay, Gerry,' I said. 'Where was he?'

'Down the street,' she said.

'You said that,' I said. 'And Mum is upstairs now, so you can tell me where he really was, for down the street just means you didn't want to say.'

'He was in the shelters with Oxfam and a few beer cans,' she said. 'Then they sloped off behind the Buildings.'

'Oh,' I said.

The Buildings is an old rickety pavilion, on the Sea Road, opposite the Prom. It used to be a cinema and then it was a roller rink and then it was a furniture store and then it was an Amusement Arcade, and now it is just the Buildings. There are five shops along the front of it, a newsagent's and a Jehovah's Witness place and three candyfloss and icecream joints that open up in summer, and round the back there is a square of land that is used for a funfair, and beyond that again is the bungalow. When Gerry said 'behind the Buildings' I knew that she meant he was going to the bungalow.

With cans of beer.

And Oxfam!

Oxfam Taylor is in the pretty-pills-and-glue brigade.

'What was Phil going there for?'

'He looked tight to me,' she said.

'Drunk?' I said.

'Well, neither of them was very steady,' she said.

'Oh God!' I said. 'I've ruined his life!' I was only half joking.

The bungalow isn't a bungalow any more. It has gone to pot like the rest of the Buildings. It's more a shack on stilts, with the windows bashed in and the doors hanging open. The likes of Oxfam and Willie Spence and Brenda Keegan and the glue-sniffing ones hang out there. I don't know exactly what they *do* there on a cold winter night, because I've never been. I never would, nobody would who wanted to keep a whole skin and a small town reputation. There's dossers and everything there in the summer when the fair comes, but in the winter it's strictly for the local winos.

'Funny class of person you knock about with, Big Sister,' Gerry said.

'No, I don't,' I said, and I told her what had happened ... my version that is, I'm sure Phil would tell it differently.

'So he's taken to drink for his broken heart,' Gerry said.

'Mrs M. will have kittens, and it's all down to me!' I said.

'No, it isn't,' she said. 'It's down to Phil.'

'Oh hell!' I said, and I went out to the hall and put on my disaster coat.

'Frankie?' Gerry said.

'Shut up or you'll have Mum down on us,' I said.

'But ...'

'Just you look after the Benefit Book till I'm back,' I said, making a joke of it, and at the same time exiting through the front door without squeaking it, which is a knack that takes some doing with our front door.

Gerry came after me, shrugging her coat on. I didn't *want* her to. It was none of her business.

'You know what you're doing?' she said. 'You're messing in other people's lives, as usual!'

'That's up to me, isn't it?' I said.

'If Phil Moore wants to hang out with that load of

junkies you should let him do it,' she said.

'I'm going to get hold of him and tell him to wise up,' I said, determinedly. The thing was I knew the Moore set-up, she didn't. Mrs M. and Phil were at daggers drawn anyway ... a lot of that was over *me* ... and Phil getting drunk with Oxfam, or worse, could lead to all kinds of ructions.

'You can't go to the bungalow, Frankie,' Gerry said, falling in step beside me. 'You know you can't.'

'We'll see about that,' I said.

If *she* didn't think I could, then I *could* and I *would*, that was the thought in my head, and at the same time another part of me was saying that I was daft, because Phil *was* none of my business any more, and it would be a good laugh if his Mum went up the wall and started throwing the crockery about. Still, it was sort-of my fault, because of the way I'd cut him at the shelters, just walking off on him like that. I didn't think he'd throw an act over me ... it was flattering in a way, but it also gave me a daft sense of obligation.

We crossed over the road and up Church Lane to the Tech, and then we headed down the Main Street, past the bank.

'Look,' Gerry said. 'You're not going to the bungalow, for I won't let you.'

'I am,' I said.

'This is going to be another of your Big Scenes!' she said, disgustedly.

Look who is talking, I thought.

'*Frankie?*' she said.

'Buzz off,' I said.

'I will not buzz off,' she said.

'Okay, don't then,' I said. 'But don't interfere!'

26

And all the time I was conscious that what I was doing was daft, and mad, rushing through the snow to rescue wronged love, and she was right, it was a Big Act, but I wasn't the one who did the Big Acts, she was.

There's a part of me enjoying this I thought. Maybe little sister was right.

'You can't go down to the bungalow!' Geraldine said, for the second time, as we came over the bridge. 'Here, hold on a bit till I see who is in the café that might help us.'

She went into Rudi's.

Rudi's is a late-night snack place, the only one that stays open at night in the winter along the Sea Road. There are lots of them that open up every summer, people who buy up the franchises with their redundancy money, and then go bust after the first season, but Rudi has the trade all to himself in winter ... what there is of it, which isn't much apart from Saturday nights when they line their cars up in the street outside after closing time, and leave chicken carcases rotting in the rain. The farmers and the country people do that ... though why they want to sit in their cars on our Sea Road on winter's nights is beyond me ... you'd think they'd have beds to go to. Rudi's real name isn't Rudi. It is Winston Campbell, after Winston Churchill, but he thought Winston didn't sound right for a trattoria. It isn't a trattoria anyway so I don't know what he was on about. Perhaps he thought it was going to be a trattoria, and then when the Coke sign and the Seven Up and the talking mechanical parrot and the fryer and the fishbox were installed, that was that ... another dream gone sour in the New Economy. Rudi's is Rudi's, all plastic flowers and chicken suppers and Page Three calendars. Winston has a red, white and blue apron, and a picture of the Queen and Prince Philip above the fish fryer, overlapping the grease vent.

When Gerry came out of Rudi's, Patrick Hagen was with her.

I was mad at her for involving him, and he didn't look too pleased!

'We need you because you are big and strong and we are helpless wee ladies!' Geraldine told him, and she wrapped herself onto his arm and flashed her hair in his face, dragging him along. I felt like apologising to him, but that would only have made it worse. I could have kicked her!

'Down there?' Patrick said, peering into the darkness.

We were at the end of the Buildings, where the entry goes down between the Buildings and the Hotel to the back, on the way across the field to the bungalow.

'Just go down there and see if my mad sister's boyfriend is there, Patrick,' Geraldine said. 'If he is ... If he is, tell him our Frankie is up here, and she wants to see him urgently.'

'You'll tell him no such thing!' I said, hot and bothered, because the whole thing was getting worse. I didn't want Gerry in it, or Patrick Hagen ... I wasn't even sure that I wanted to be in it myself.

'If we don't say that, he'll not come,' Gerry said.

'I think you are both nuts,' Patrick said. 'You know that place. Phil Moore wouldn't go there.'

'I saw him, Patrick,' Gerry said, and she gave him one of her wheedling looks.

Patrick gave in: Just like Patrick, I thought, always being used by other people. If it wasn't his awful family thrusting every little thing onto him—he's the *respectable* Hagen, the one who doesn't go getting tight and shouting at policemen—if it wasn't them, it was us ... well, Geraldine really, putting the hex on him her usual way ... but I

28

couldn't get out of it entirely. It was my Phil who was the cause of all the trouble.

We started down the alley, working our way through the gate beneath the concrete box on stilts that jutted out over it. It used to be the projection box, and there was a ladder leading up to it, but the ladder went years ago, when the cinema closed. God alone knows what lives up there now! The cinema had to close because of Cinemascope, my Dad says. It was too narrow to take the big screen, and all you could see was a little strip of film in the middle. Maybe that was where my Dad got the notion that you can get away with anything!

'You two wait here,' Patrick said, and we stopped, at the end of the alley, where the light from the street stopped. We could make out the shape of the bungalow roof against the hedge behind it, but only just.

'I don't suppose one of you has a torch?' Patrick said. It is a wilderness of garbage on the field, and I suppose he didn't fancy picking his way across it to the bungalow, blind, in search of stray Presbyterians.

'No,' I said.

'Well, I'll go and take a look anyway,' he said. 'Though the bungalow looks deserted to me.'

It looked deserted to me as well, but then I suppose it would. They have old boxes and things up against the broken windows, to stop the cops and ordinary human beings seeing in. Everybody knows what goes on there, in a general sort of way, but at least when it goes on down there we don't have to know the particulars, and people like Oxfam Grant aren't throwing bricks through shop windows, or busting up the shelters.

Then, before Patrick could make his move, Geraldine said: 'Patrick!' just like that.

She stopped in her tracks.

She was staring down at the ground, next to her, by the end of the alley wall.

There was something huddled there, on the ground.

Somebody.

Some *body*.

I had this idea in my head, just a flash. The Provos leave bodies like that, sometimes, all wired up. Boobytrapped. The police are meant to come and look and BOOM ... no cop, no corpse, just another bloody blancmange on the ground, another blow for Ireland!

'Don't touch it!' I said, grabbing at Patrick's coat.

IT.

IT was a HIM.

A man.

He was lying against the alley wall, on a pile of garbage, hunched over, face down. There was snow on him, and his trouser leg was rucked up, showing a grey and black and red sock.

'Holy-Mother-of-God!' said Patrick, shakily.

Chapter 4

I was really scared, there in the dark alley, with a dead body at my feet.

But the man wasn't dead.

When Patrick touched him, a kind of wheeze rumbled up from his chest, and a dribble came out of his mouth. It might have been vomit. I don't know what it was, spittle maybe.

I don't know how Patrick did it. I wouldn't have. I couldn't have. Or maybe I could. I suppose I would have touched him if I'd been all alone, if I'd had to.

His face was whitey-blue, but the blue was probably the cold. There was snow on his hair. He had a snazzy red tie, and some of his shirt buttons were opened. He had a tatty vest, all smeared with whatever had come out of his mouth.

'Get a bloody doctor or an ambulance or something!' Patrick said, bending down beside the man.

'Shouldn't we ...'

'Go on! Do it!' Patrick said.

Gerry and I went running up the alley, out onto the Sea Road.

It wasn't exactly packed with doctors and ambulances.

'Phone!' I said.

'Where?' said Gerry. She was all shiny-eyed with excitement.

'Winston Campbell's phone!' I said, and we belted down

31

the road towards Rudi's, but we didn't get there, because on the way we remembered the box outside the Post Office, and that meant that we didn't have to go any further.

Geraldine was first in the box, so she dialled nine-nine-nine. It seemed a funny thing to be dialling. I never dialled it before. I didn't get dialling it this time either. She did.

'Emergency Services,' the telephone said to her. 'What service do you require?'

'There's a man lying down behind the Buildings on the Sea Road and he looks like he's dying,' Geraldine said, and the somebody on the other end asked her something else and she said: 'This is an anonymous call!' and put the receiver down.

'What did you do that for?' I asked, astonished.

'So they won't know it is us,' she said.

I grabbed the telephone from her.

'What are you doing?'

'I'm not messing about!' I said, and I dialled nine-nine-nine myself.

I told them who I was and where I was and why I was calling and said would they come quick because the man looked to me like he was still breathing, but only just.

I think the woman believed me.

'Now you've landed us in it!' Gerry said.

'Trust you to lose the bap!' I retorted.

Honestly, our Geraldine has no wit sometimes.

'Come on,' I said, starting back towards the Buildings.

'No way!' she said, hanging back.

'Don't be daft,' I said.

'I'm not getting mixed up in trouble,' she said.

'We are mixed up,' I said.

'You are,' she said. 'I'm not.'

32

'You silly kid!' I said, amazed at her.

'I'm staying put,' she said.

'You do that then,' I said. 'I'm going back. Patrick might need me.'

I turned and I ran back up the road to the alley at the side of the Buildings.

Patrick wasn't there.

Nobody was.

Except the man.

He was still lying down.

I couldn't go down the alley near him. I was too afraid.

I just stood there on the corner, waiting for things to start happening, and that's where I was when the cops came.

One of them got out of the car and came towards me.

'He's down there,' I said, pointing down the alley.

'Who is?'

'The man is,' I said.

The cop flashed his light down the alley.

The man was there, all right.

Two other cops spilled out of the car, and the one who stayed in got on the radio.

'Who're you?' one of the cops asked.

I told him who I was, and where I came from.

'Oh, aye?' he said. He knew as well as I did what my address meant.

The two other cops went down the alley ... one in front, the other twenty paces back.

'Unity Park?' my cop said. 'You're out late.'

'Yes,' I said.

'On your own?' he said.

'Yes,' I said, knowing it was a lie, but I couldn't figure out what else to say.

One of the other cops came running up the alley, over to the car. He started talking on the radio.

My cop went over to them.

I didn't know what I was supposed to do. I just stood there.

Another cop came from the car.

'Miss Rafferty?' he said.

'Yes.'

'It looks like your man has had a heart attack,' he said. 'But don't you be running off now. Stay put, till we've time to talk to you.'

Then the ambulance came.

It must have fairly blistered down the Fortwilliam Road. You could hear it coming a mile off, even with the sea breaking on the promenade wall, over the way.

The cops had fanned out round the alley. One of them was with the man, and another was standing near him, by the wall, but looking the other way, into the darkness of the field. Another was up near me, but he wasn't watching me, he was watching the road.

They were acting easy, but they weren't. I knew why, but I didn't want to think about it. In case there was someone waiting for a soft shot, that was why, and my presence won't have been any comfort on that score, coming from where I did, Bandit Territory. I thought for a moment about the old projection box, overhead, and then I just blanked the thought out of me.

'Maybe you'd like to wait in the car, Miss Rafferty?' the cop at the car called out to me.

'Okay, yes,' I said.

And I went over and got in the back of the car.

'You sit tight there, love,' he said.

He didn't look any older than me.

34

The ambulancemen got weaving with their stretcher, and meanwhile a few more cops turned up. There was a whole Conference of them, and nobody paying any attention to me.

I felt like I'd been arrested.

Patrick and Gerry had let me down. One minute there were three of us, and the next there was just me, hauled in by the cops. Typical Gerry.

I was going to give them a right telling off.

The ambulance pulled off.

A policeman came over and tapped the window, and I got out of the car.

He asked me my name and address, and took it down.

'You found him?' he said.

'Yes.'

'And you telephoned?'

'Yes.'

'Do you know who he is, love?'

'No,' I said. 'Who is he?'

'Search me!' the cop said. Then he asked what I was doing there.

'Just out for a walk,' I said.

'Down *there*?'

'Well, I was looking for somebody,' I said.

'Yes?' he said.

'This is not going to get me into any trouble, is it?' I said. 'I mean I was only trying to help. And ... and I saw him there and I saw he was ill or something and I went and rang, that's all.'

'Why would you get into trouble?' he said.

I could have told him that anybody from down our way knows the cops *get* you into trouble. People from Unity Park don't go talking to cops. Getting you into trouble is what cops are there for. Well, sort of. I *know* that that isn't right, but it is the way that our people feel.

'If there is any trouble,' I said.

'You did very well,' he said, reassuringly. 'You've nothing to worry about. Just tell me what happened.'

I suppose he must have seen that I was on edge. He was quite decent really, for a cop.

'I was just out for a walk and I ... and I thought I heard something ... like a dog, hurt or something ... and I went and I looked and I found him,' I said, wondering why I was lying.

I hadn't time to think it out ... so I said the first thing that came into my mind. And a hurt dog was reasonable, wasn't it?

The Unity Park way of thinking had got me, that's what it was! All the stories about the police laying into people—that would be why Patrick cleared off, any road. If the cops found a Hagen from Unity Park hanging round anything they'd beat a confession to *something* out of him—and I was just as bad as he was, thinking that way!

'Maybe we'd better run you up the road, love,' the cop said. He'd closed his book. He didn't seem all that interested in what I was saying. So maybe I was getting worked up all over nothing.

'Oh, no, I'll walk,' I said, because the last thing on God's Earth I wanted was a squad car rolling up at the door, full of armed-to-the-teeth cops, and Frankie Rafferty coming bowling out of it into her Mammy's lap! A Late Late Show appearance like that would be one that I'd never live down.

'Are you finished with me now?' I said.

'We'll be in touch,' he said. 'Thank you, love.'

I'm not your love, I felt like telling him, but he didn't mean it that way. He was quite human, really. Wife and two kids and mortgage human, that is. He looked tired. It's difficult thinking of cops as people, when you come from down our way. Dad says that the cops are the way you treat them, and he never treated them bad and they never said a bad word to him. Belly Kelly would tell you different from his Civil Rights days, but then that was the old long-time-ago cops, and even the Belly says there's a change, though he says you never know what you'd find underneath if you scratched one.

It's all a big muddle, the thing about the cops. Even the don't-want-to-shoot-people lot, the S.D.L.P., the ones that talk to the British, even they won't back the cops all the way, because they say there are cops and cops, and some of the cops are still hard men dressed up. The reality of it is that it's difficult for anybody on the Catholic side to say yes to the cops, when there is so much old history of the cops bashing people, and so much new talk about them still doing it. And whether they do that or not, the Provos still shoot them.

So do the Loyalists now, but they don't shoot the cops so often. They petrol bomb the cops' houses, instead.

I suppose if I was a cop with both lots ready to shoot me I might beat in the odd head, on the offchance that it was the right one! The cops must be really scared, a lot of the time, and I suppose that that doesn't help. The same thing goes for the U.D.R. and the soldiers. I'd be dead panicky, patrolling round in a flak jacket waiting to be shot at. It's not surprising that they shoot first, some of the time, but not a very comforting thought to live with, either.

I think if you treat them right they're probably all right, like my Dad said, but I don't know.

I went straight home down the street.

Gerry was downstairs when I came in.

'Mum's mad!' she said.

'That makes two of us,' I said. 'For I'm mad with you! What did you go and tell her?'

'I didn't tell her anything,' she said. 'It all came over on the bush telegraph!'

Mum came down the stairs, in her dressing-gown.

'Well, Frankie?' she said.

'Well, I'm back,' I said.

'Mrs Harty was in,' she said. 'Her Micky was down the road. He told her the whole thing, and she came round to see did I know.'

'Well, there you are now,' I said. Trust Micky Harty to be in on it! He must have spotted me at the cop car, on his way back from the pub.

'I'm not too pleased,' Mum said.

'Well, neither am I,' I said. 'But I'm too tired to talk about it. If you want to make a row, we can have it in the morning!'

And I just left her there, and went off up the stairs to my room. I used to share it with Gerry, but she has the spare room now. She said she couldn't share with me any more, because I was too hysterical after my Dad left. She's no call to say I'm hysterical—not what I'd call hysterical anyway. When I lose the bap, I've good cause for it.

Gerry didn't say much when she came up, and neither did I.

I hadn't the strength to tell her off.

She just said, 'You are for the high jump when she gets you in the morning!' in a cheerful sort of way, and we left it at that. She went off to her room.

Me in my room, Gerry in hers, and Mum downstairs watching the old T.V. drag on ... and no Dad.

It used to be so different. Dad was the one it all revolved

around. We used to go for walks up the mountain, the three of us, and he would show Gerry and me plants and ferns and things, and how to get under the waterfall. We got on fine, and I remember being happy.

I lay in bed thinking about that, and wondering what had happened to me, because to begin with I was the strong one, helping Mum, and sorting Gerry out, but it had gone wrong, somehow. A strange thing had happened. I was the strong one, but now they were treating me as if I was a nervous case, a bit off my rocker, someone who needed protecting.

I didn't feel like that sort of person, but what I felt and what I *did* were different things. What I was doing, bit by bit, was cutting myself off from them all.

Chapter 5

The next morning was supposed to be the Gunfight at the O.K. Corral, restaged in number 17 Unity Close, when Mum sat down and read me a lecture about sneaking off and getting into trouble with the police ... not that I'd been in trouble with the police, but I'd never convince her of that. Mum doesn't listen when she's in that mood.

It didn't work out that way.

Mrs Hagen slipped in the snow, or what was left of it, which wasn't much because it was a bright clear morning, and the snow had begun to melt.

It could have happened to anybody, but of course it happened to her. She wasn't carrying stolen goods stuffed up her jumper, or celebrating getting Danny home from the police, or any of the usual Hagen things. The cops were charging Danny with a list of thieving as long as your arm, and doing Mrs Hagen for assault and obstruction, so there wasn't much to celebrate anyway! She was just out walking her wee Brendan on his trike.

Wham! goes Brendan on his trike, right into the back of her leg.

Mrs Hagen gave a yowl, slipped, and ended up on her back in the sludge, with her left leg folded under her.

Twice in twenty-four hours I got ringing for an ambulance.

This one took a bit longer coming, and when it did I

wound up looking after Brendan Hagen, and my Mum went off in the back of it, holding Mrs Hagen's hand. I don't see why Mum had to go, and neither did anybody else except Mrs Hagen, who kept on about how she wasn't a well woman, and she'd never be back, and she needed somebody there with her in the hospital, somebody who knew her and could talk to the doctors and sort out what was what. She seemed to think they'd make away with her, if she hadn't got a witness to take her side. Nobody could find Daddy Hagen, and Danny was off somewhere, probably working out some alibis, and nobody else came leaping out of the wallpaper except the Belly Kelly, and he is too old and fat to go riding in ambulances. So my Mum ended up sticking on her dealing-with-officialdom hat, packing Mrs Hagen's spare nighties, and riding off in the ambulance.

I was standing there watching it go off, when Con McCluskey came up to me.

'See you, Frankie?' he said.

'Yes, Con?' I said.

'You want to watch yourself,' he said.

'Oh?' I said, because I didn't know what he was getting at.

'Chatting to the R.U.C.,' he said.

Obviously Teresa Harty had been up to tell him what her brother Micky had seen. It doesn't take long for word to get about on Unity Park.

'You're growing up to be a bad bitch, Frankie,' he said.

I just stared at him. He said it coldly. He was standing close to me, looking me in the eye.

I don't know what I did. I stood and stared at him. The Belly Kelly must have twigged what was going on. He came lumbering over.

'Young Con?' he said.

Con nodded, but he never took his eyes off me.

'Clear off and leave the girl alone,' the Belly said.

'What do you know about it, Kelly?' Con said. Con is thin and small and beardy, one of those wiry, intense people. He's quiet, and soft spoken, which is one reason why the 'bad bitch' line threw me a bit. He doesn't say things like that.

'Clear off and leave the girl alone, Con,' the Belly repeated.

'Just so long as she gets the message,' Con said, and he turned away.

He went over to Teresa Harty, and stood talking to her on the corner, with his back to us.

'Wait a bit ... ' I said, moving to go after him.

The Belly stopped me.

'Never mind him, daughter,' the Belly said. It was meant to be reassurance. I don't know if I was reassured.

Round our way Con is the Easter Revolution and the Thirty-two County Socialist Republic all wrapped up in one person. He's never liked me, not since the time I was at a party in his house and I went for one of his mates. I don't remember what it was all about. This man called Pearce was there and he was blowing about the Armed Struggle and whatnot, and it was soon after Bob Allen got shot. I more or less told him that nobody wanted a United Ireland if it was all going to be drenched in the blood of people who didn't believe in it, and there was a hell of a row.

I went on the blacklist then, and apparently I'd notched up a few more points for myself.

Gerry came up.

'What did Con say to you?' she said.

42

I told her.

'Jesus!' she said. 'You don't deserve that.'

'I haven't done anything,' I said.

'Watch yourself,' she said. 'You know what people are like around here.'

Well, I do, and I don't. I know what the Hartys and the Hagens and the Curlys and the rent-a-mob are like, but they are the kind you find anywhere, who latch onto any old trouble. What I don't know about is the other lot, the people Con mixes with. They're not in the stone throwing business, and they don't advertise, but they make things happen.

Bob Allen type things.

I should never even have gone to that party. I don't know what got into me. I told Pearce that the Provos were a bunch of Fascists, when he was making out that they were Marxist Revolutionaries. I shouted a whole lot about the Starry Plough flag they had pinned up over the mantelpiece, with them all singing boozy songs around it. In the end Pearce's girlfriend went for me, and I'd have been in wee pieces if Con McCluskey hadn't got me out of the house, and walked me back to our place.

He didn't say a lot that time, either, but somehow the not saying a lot was more impressive than the shouting, arguing lot he'd left behind him. Pearce was just thick, and a big mouth, but Con really believes in what he's doing ... whatever it is ... his whole life is caught up and committed to it, and he doesn't *want* to understand that not everybody is like that.

Con would kill, if he had to, for all the quiet softness about him. He wouldn't if he didn't have to, he's not a cowboy, but doing it wouldn't hurt him inside. The quietness is a shell that has formed round whatever has happened inside him, whatever it is that can make a political idea matter so much. That is the one really frightening thing you have to hand to people like Con ... they do it for the *idea*, not for glory, not because they're paid to do it. They do frightful things, and take frightful risks, and it is all about the idea. I'm not saying the Provisional I.R.A. are all like that, because they're not, but I know Con *is*, and there's plenty more like him. If there wasn't the whole thing would be so much simpler. How do you cope with somebody who genuinely gets hold of an idea and is prepared to die for it? Hunt them and kill them? Then they're martyrs, and the black-edged mass cards and the mourners and the rifles over the grave all get going the seeds of other martyrdoms.

It's daft and crazy and I don't want to know about it.

I was left on the pavement, looking after Brendan Hagen and his trike.

We trundled back to the house, and I was just figuring how I'd share the child-minding for the day with Gerry, when I realised that she'd cleared off, and left me to do it alone!

'Big deal!' I told wee Brendan. 'I hope some of your family show up soon!'

There were no Hagens about their house, and all I could do was hope. Patrick was off on his bin lorry, Eamonn was locked up somewhere in need of care and protection ... although we were the ones that needed protecting from him ... Danny was doing his alibis ... and Maureen and Roisin were too small. That left the Daddy Hagen and a calculation about the odds on finding him sober. It was past eleven o'clock, and the most likely place to find him was down on the sand dunes with his Beach Club, and their carry-out bags from the Off-Licence, so I didn't go searching.

'Looks like you and me for the day, Brendan!' I said.

I went over to the Hagens' ... Mrs H. had given me the key ... and I picked up a tin of beans for him. Then I went back to our house and made him the beans.

'There you are!' I said. 'Eat that up!' and I gave him some bread and marg, and a drink of orange juice.

'Thank you very much,' he said, and started eating.

He was a mucky eater.

Half the beans ended up on the kitchen floor.

'You're a messer,' I told him, and I got the brush and pan and cleared it up. Then I went to put the beans in the pedal bin and found it was overflowing ... so much for the housekeeping in our house ... so I took the rubbish bag out to our back to dump in the bin.

Somebody had been busy in our back.

There were things about me written on the wall of the shed, in great big white letters. Me and the cops. As if I was *in* with the cops, or something!

The paint was still sticky.

I was really mad.

It must have been the young Curlys, or the Hartys, or one of those. Some of them had come over our back fence and written it up, probably when everybody was out the front looking after Mrs Hagen.

I got one of my Dad's brushes out of the shed, and tried to spread the words about, but it didn't really work, and there was no paint stripper.

I had to get the writing off the wall before my Mum came back.

I went into the house again, and got my coat, then I grabbed hold of wee Brendan.

45

'Come on, wee Brendan,' I told him. 'We're going to the shop.'

'Get me a sweetie,' he said, brightening up.

'Well, maybe,' I said.

I went out, banging the door behind me.

There were three or four of them standing down at the end of the Close, on the other side.

I went by them with never a look.

Nobody said anything, but they must all have known.

I felt really *hot* inside, all bubbly. I was down to the road when it came to me that I was doing the wrong thing, dashing off like that. They'd maybe come up and do the front of the house, when I was out, and anyway the thing was to get the message off, and the best way I could do that was to paint over it, and there was paint in the shed.

'Back home, Brendan,' I told him.

'What about the sweeties?' he said.

'You'll get your sweeties later,' I said.

Coming back up the Park I could see the young ones still on the corner where I'd left them. I came slowly, because I wasn't going to give them the satisfaction of seeing I was put out.

One of them shouted something, but I didn't hear what it was.

Then I turned into the Close.

There was a van outside our house, and a man getting out of it.

It was my Dad.

He must have had someone on the look-out, so he could come when the house was empty.

I went all cold inside.

He tried to use his key to get in, but he couldn't.

Mum had the locks changed, just for that reason.

He didn't see me. He went to the window, and had a look in, and all the time I was walking up behind him, so he had a real shock coming, and I was going to give it to him!

He turned round, and he saw me.

Caught in the act!

'Hullo,' I said to my Dad.

'Frankie,' he said, looking put out. He glanced towards the van. There was another man in the van, a man I didn't know, and an old greyhound in a cage thing in the back.

'Yes,' I said. 'Remember me, do you?'

'How are you?' he said.

'Brilliant,' I said, standing there in my disaster coat, my hand clamped onto wee Brendan. The way I said it was meant to skewer him! Just dead, no feeling in it. I wouldn't give him the satisfaction.

The wee lads on the corner of the Close were watching us, all eager for a laugh. I wouldn't give them the satisfaction either.

'Frankie ... ?' he said. He didn't know where to put himself, with me arriving in the middle to bust up his burglarising act.

'Yes?'

'How is your mother?' he managed.

'Brilliant,' I said. 'She's brilliant too.'

There was a long pause.

'And how is Mrs Evans?' I said.

Mrs Evans is the lady from the supermarket cheese counter that he ran off with, to wherever he ran off to.

'Fine,' he said.

'That's brilliant as well,' I said. 'You can tell her that from me. Tell I think it is just brilliant that she is fine and dandy and I hope it chokes her.'

'Frankie ...' he said.

'Frankie-Frankie-Frankie,' I said, mimicking him.

'Och, hell! Give me a chance, Frankie!' he said.

'Don't you curse at me,' I told him.

'I just came by to pick up some of my old things,' he said, limply.

'Well you can just go away without them,' I said. 'Get in your wee van with your wee friend and his wee dog and motor off out of here before ... before ...'

'Och, Frankie!' he said.

His eyes had gone all wet, and there was a big flush up the side of his face.

'Go to hell, you!' I shouted at him, losing the bap. 'It's your word. It is where you belong. You and your *brilliant* woman!'

'I can't talk to you like this, Frankie,' he said, and he turned and went back to the van. The crowd on the corner stirred, interested. He got in, and then he wound the window down.

'I love you all the same, Frankie,' he said.

'Brilliant!' I said.

I turned my head away from him, so he wouldn't see my face.

I heard the van start, and move off.

'Sweeties?' Brendan said, tugging my hand.

'You're getting no sweeties!' I said.

Somebody shouted something, from the crowd at the corner. I turned round, and gave them the fingers, with my face all wet.

They laughed, Sean and Colum Curly, Dominic Harty

48

and the young McCann one.

'Come on, Brendan,' I said, and I unlocked the door and dragged him in. The ones outside were shouting things at me, but I paid no heed.

I flopped down on the sofa.

My Dad wasn't going sneaking round our house when we were all out to see if there were any pickings left over from the Holy-Sacrament-of-Marriage-Made-in-Heaven-Let-No-Man-Put-Asunder- Unless-He-has-a-Mrs-Evans-to-turn-to. Anyroad, there wasn't much of his left. Mum even tore up his crossword book.

I don't know my Dad's Mrs Evans. She was supposed to be on the cheese counter, but I can't remember seeing anybody there but a man in a white hat, and a red striped apron, with dirty fingernails.

Maybe he was Mr Evans.

Maybe it was the fingernails put her off him.

My Dad always had clean nails. He was fussy, like that. It is a pity he wasn't so fussy when it came round to sniffing round Mr Evans's wife, and dumping his own children!

'Want sweeties!' said Brendan.

'Shut up!' I said.

He stuck his thumb in his mouth, and stood there looking at me.

In desperation, I got him a biscuit.

'Eat that!' I said.

Buzzing round in my mind was the thought that Dad had asked after me, and he'd asked after Mum, but he hadn't asked after Gerry, and she was always the favourite. I reckoned he *knew* how she was, that was the only way to explain it.

Maybe she was the one who had tipped him off that

the house was empty.

I knew that couldn't be right, because she wasn't around ... where was she?

Just then I could have done with her, or somebody, anybody ... but there was nobody, only Brendan and his biscuit and his dirty bean mess I still hadn't wiped properly, and the paint mess on the shed.

It was all a mess. My whole life was.

And it was down to my Dad.

It was no good him standing there caught out on his burglar trip, crying at me with his face all red.

I was crying myself now but it was all right, because there was only wee Brendan to see me and he didn't know any different. I might have been crying over anything.

It was my Dad I was crying over. What I'd done to him, and what he'd done to me.

Chapter 6

Patrick Hagen arrived at the house about four o'clock, looking sheepish. By the look of him he was straight off his bin lorry.

Nobody else had been near me.

Not surprisingly, by the time he arrived on the doorstep I was feeling a bit sour. I'd spent my time painting out the words on the shed wall as best I could, and entertaining Brendan Hagen, all the time rehearsing what I should have said to my Dad and hadn't.

'I've come for our Brendan,' he said. 'The Belly Kelly told me he was here.'

'The Belly is a great old listening post,' I said, and I let him in.

It was fresh in my mind that I had a bone to pick with Patrick, as well as the rest of the world. He had cleared off and left me to deal with the sick man down the alley, and the cops.

I'd only let him through the door, but Brendan must have heard his voice, for he came charging out and launched himself at Patrick's middle, like a dive-bomber. Patrick scooped him up, and swung him round. I had fears for the wallpaper from the flying heels.

'Here now, Brendy!' he said. 'Will I give you a burley?'

'Give it to him in the front room!' I said.

Patrick got Brendan by the arms and swung the child

out from his body, round and round and round, till Brendan started shrieking to be let down.

'You'll have him in tears,' I said.

'Not me!' said Patrick. 'Me and Brendy are two pals. Aren't we, Brendan?'

'Yeah!' said Brendan, all red in the face and puffy.

'Well, I'm glad some of your family turned up at last,' I said. 'I was beginning to think Brendan had moved in for good.'

'It was good of your Ma,' Patrick said. He had his donkey-jacket on, with the orange shoulder pads and the District Council logo on the back. His bin gloves stuck out of his pocket.

'Your mother was in a bad way,' I said. 'I mean, I'm sure she'll be all right, but there is no doubt she took a bad knock. That is what the ambulanceman said, anyway.'

Then I thought I would bowl it at him, for I wasn't over being left on my oney-o the night before.

'It was the same ambulanceman as last night,' I said. 'They must work long shifts.'

Patrick made a face.

'Yeah,' he said. 'Well, you know the way things are?'

'Oh, *sure*,' I said.

'Me and the cops don't get on, like,' he said.

'*Dirty* cops,' said Brendan. 'Bang-bang-bang!' and he made a gun of his hand, bouncing round.

Patrick looked at him, and then he looked at me. He didn't say anything. I wasn't surprised, really. The child had picked it up from the talk around him, and you couldn't expect the Hagens to love the R.U.C., exactly, when they were forever getting themselves arrested.

'The cops took Mammy,' Brendan said, suddenly looking anxious. He came over to Patrick, and clung onto his knee.

Patrick hugged him. 'The cops took Mammy, and they'll put her away in prison like our Eamonn.'

'No, they won't, Brendy,' Patrick said. 'Nobody is going to hurt your Mammy.'

'Mammy's gone,' Brendan said.

'She hurted herself,' Patrick said. 'She'll be all right. The good doctors in the hospital will put your Mammy's leg right. She's not away at all. She'll be back home soon.'

'Our Eamonn isn't coming back home,' Brendan said, and he stuck his thumb in his mouth.

'Eamonn's all right,' Patrick said.

I could have told him Eamonn was all *wrong*, but I didn't bother my head. The thing he finally got put away for was breaking and entering Flynn's garage for cigarettes and stuff ... they found the takings in the roof space at Hagens' ... although Mrs Hagen tried to make out it was all for the Cause, and her Eamonn was an Irish Martyr. I doubt if the Provos would have had any use for him, for Eamonn was a wild one. It's not the wild ones they *can* use, and there are enough recruits about so they can afford to be choosy. Every time a Provo gets shot, or there's a hunger strike or whatnot, the recruits come diving in. If the Provos used those like Eamonn they wouldn't be in business long, and the fact that they are still in business is enough to show that it isn't the likes of Eamonn Hagen or the Hartys that get recruited ... it's the bright ones, the ones who can think for themselves, who get the bug. They see the Brits and the U.D.R. and the English soldiers and the R.U.C. and the rifles, and they see only one thing ... the enemy that has to be got rid of. By their way of thinking, if the Brits go it will be a whole new ball game ... though if you ask me that is just when the whole shooting works would fall apart. While the Brits are there, there is something to fight against. If the Brits went, then we'd be down to war amongst ourselves, against the Protestants first, and then *if* they managed to kill off the Protestants, against the rest of Ireland, which is conservative and and Bless-me-Father to a man ... some hopes there of a Marxist Revolution! That's if they ever got rid of the Protestants ... but the Protestants aren't going to go either. They're as mad and bad as our lot, except most of the time they've never had to bother, because since there was a Northern Ireland, since Partition in the 1920s, their violence has been the licensed, official kind ... take away the licence, make them into the revolutionaries against a Thirty-two County Republic, and you'd have as big a problem as you have with the I.R.A.

It's all a jar of worms.

'You cleared off on me last night!' I said to Patrick, not-just-going-to-let-him-away with it, because I was in no mood to let anybody away with anything, after the paint on the shed and my Dad doing his burglar bit. I wanted somebody's blood!

'I didn't want to stick around,' he said. 'The man was sick. There was nothing I could do for him.'

'That's a fine attitude!' I said.

'I told you, I don't talk to cops,' he said.

'Well, I don't either,' I said.

There was an awkward silence.

'You wouldn't need to,' he said.

'Meaning?' I said.

'You should have cleared off,' he said. 'Your Gerry cleared off.'

'I gave my name over the telephone,' I said, wishing I hadn't, and wondering if I would have cleared off, if I hadn't. 'Anyway, the man was sick. I thought you were staying to help him, and I was coming back to help you.'

'Catch yourself on!' he said.

'The cops couldn't have touched you, if you'd stayed, Patrick,' I said.

'You tell that to the cops,' I said.

'I don't know any cops,' I said.

He didn't believe me! I *knew* he didn't, although he never said a word.

'Where's all this talk about me coming from?' I burst out. 'I never talked to a cop in my life before, hardly, till last night, and the way everybody is going on you'd think I'd . . . I'd . . .'

'Your Da wasn't too choosy with his friends,' Patrick said.

I gaped at him.

'Your Da had one or two *friends* in the Force,' he said, and the way he said *friends* didn't make it seem friendly at all.

'My Dad's a Socialist!' I said. It was a funny thing to say, because in a way, to someone like Patrick, it didn't mean anything at all.

'My Dad was on the marches, and he nearly got arrested!' I said. He was too, in the Civil Rights like old Belly, before the whole thing erupted. After that, he gave up.

'There's some people say that your Da said a thing or two too much,' Patrick said.

'Meaning?' I said.

'I'm not saying it,' Patrick said, realising he'd gone too far. 'But I'm only telling you for your own good. You want to watch yourself, if you are going to live around here. Your Da is maybe better off out of it.'

'Are you saying that my Dad was an *informer*?' I said.

'Nobody said that,' Patrick said. 'Not to me, anyway.'

'But they do say, amongst themselves?' I said.

'I don't know what *they* say now, do I?' said Patrick.

Informer is just about the most dangerous thing you can say about anybody, where we are. People who inform end up dead in ditches. People they even think *might* be informing end up that way too. It is one way of keeping the organisation intact, and the footsoldiers in line.

'My Dad never had anything to do with the likes of that,' I said, wondering would he have, if he *had* known something? If he'd known who shot Bob Allen, for instance, would my Dad have gone to the police?

I didn't know. I really and truly didn't know. He *might*, I suppose, if it was Bob Allen, because Bob Allen was a decent man, and my Dad was decent too ... and why wouldn't he tell the police, if he knew who it was that shot Bob Allen? It would be the right thing to do, wouldn't it?

Not if you live here! was my next thought.

Not if you want to keep a whole skin.

The thing to do here is to keep your mouth shut.

'Look, Frankie,' Patrick said. 'You ought to wise up. Because I don't know what your Da did or didn't do, but I'm only telling you he was getting a name for shooting off his mouth in some quarters, and you know as well as I do what those quarters are. You keep an eye out for yourself, that people don't start thinking the same thing about *you* ... right? If I was you, I wouldn't be seen hanging around when the cops come on the scene, just in case you get yourself blamed for anything that happens.'

'Y-e-s,' I said.

'Your Geraldine has wised up,' he said. 'She didn't hang around last night, did she?'

'No-o,' I said.

'I'm not saying I think you'd talk to the cops,' he said. 'I'm not saying I think your Da did either. I'm just saying to you to watch your step, in case other people *would* be *thinking* it, do you understand me?'

'Yes,' I said.

'Well then,' he said, uncertainly.

'I'm *not*,' I said, and I felt awful saying it, because it was a sort of cringing self-preservation creeping in, but in a way I *had* to say it, after the writing on the shed and everything. The idea was sinking in on me, slowly. If they really got it in their heads that I was talking to the cops, even though I *wasn't* ...

'I know you're not,' he said, sounding as if he didn't know it at all, he just wanted out of the house. It was very unconvincing.

'You might tell your *friends* that,' I said, knowing as I said it what a silly thing it was to say, because it sounded as if I *was*, didn't it?

'Friends?' he said.

'Con,' I said. 'Con's in and out of your house.'

'Not to see me, he's not,' Patrick said, firmly. It was probably true enough. Patrick isn't one of the mob ... he's the only Hagen who isn't. His name is probably on the blacklist too, because of it.

I said another silly thing.

'Your Ma goes round collecting for the Cause,' I said.

'That's different,' he said.

I could see the click in his mind.

There's one house they don't come round to with the collecting boxes. Three of them came one night, and my Dad shouted them from the door. Maybe that was how his name got on the books, that and knowing Bob Allen, and not being one of the enthusiasts.

'I'd better be getting back,' Patrick said, and I let him go.

I watched him through our Venetian blinds.

He went across to his own house, stopping to talk to Micky Harty on the way.

He never looked back at our house once.

Maybe he was afraid to be seen coming out of it, afraid of what they might say if they got the notion he was mixed up with me.

Dangerous to be with!

Maybe he thought I'd seduce him, and hand all his family over to the Brits!

Dangerous me ... it would have been funny, if it hadn't been *real*.

If they felt like that ... the things the kids had written on the wall, then as far as *they* were concerned I *was* dangerous.

In a place like our place everybody has to think the same thing, because the whole game relies on nobody stepping out of line.

That's why they had it in for my Dad ... my Dad who was the bloody shop steward, the one they went to when they had jobs ... but that was forgotten. Now it was my-Dad-the-big-mouth.

Like me. I should have kept my mouth shut, instead of shouting at Pearce and Con at their party.

A *suspect* person!

A part of me wanted to laugh, because it was so ridiculous. Another part was scared, really *scared*, because I knew what it could lead to.

Chapter 7

I needed somebody to talk to. Absolutely desperately I needed that somebody, but there was nobody, nobody at all, till my Mum came.

I don't know if I could have talked to my Mum. I don't think I could, really, but I didn't get the chance, because as soon as she came in she opened up a letter she'd got ... it had been sitting on the hall stand, and I'd ignored it, amid all my scenery, not knowing it was another time-bomb, waiting to go off!

It was a letter from the Welfare, telling her she had to take my Dad to court, to establish her position. She *knew* her position, so I don't know what good establishing it was supposed to do, because my Dad had no money anyway, being permanently unemployed, so it was no use dunning him, even if we had known where to find him.

No use ... but it launched her into a Litany.

'How can we go to court if the Welfare can't find him?' I asked, to drag her off it. I didn't want her on it, because I had my own guilty secret there, which was my Dad arriving at the door, when she'd been out. She was in no fit state to take that on board! I was thinking at the double-dozen because if he was still about it meant they probably *could* find him.

'I signed the papers,' she kept saying. 'I should never have signed the papers!'

'Well, I think you should!' I said.

'It's not right,' she said. 'Handing him over to them, so they can put him up in court.'

As if she were betraying him!

'They'll not find him,' I said.

Mum didn't say anything for a minute, and then she said: 'I heard he was up the back somewhere, in a shack, walking greyhounds for some man on the black.'

'Oh!' I said. It was the first I'd heard of her knowing where he was, and I was puzzled about it, because usually if she has anything to say against my Dad she lets me have it, full rip! Still, he'd got himself well organised, for once, a job on the black would keep him off the Social Security records, and he'd managed to get a house to go with it!

'I didn't want to bother you about it,' she said, awkwardly. 'I thought you might be upset!'

Hysterical me! The one who had to be protected from being *upset*, in case I blew up *again*! My Mum upset and worried over *me*. That was a laugh! I was left thinking well-if-she-knew-what-was-stuck-up-on-our-shed-wall then she'd have a lot more to be upset about ... I didn't say it, because I couldn't say it. There'd have been ructions!

'Who did you hear it from?' I said.

'Eileen Walsh,' she said.

Surprise surprise! So Mrs Walsh had been running tabs on my Dad, and never a word to me. I suppose she thought I was too *upset* to know!

'So there you are,' she said.

Then she said: 'I'm awfully sorry for him!'

You could have knocked me down with a duck feather!

'*What?*' I said, it was more of a gasp, really.

'Your Dad's not strong, you know,' she said. 'His chest.

60

A man with his chest shouldn't be out walking dogs on the mountain.'

It was really pathetic.

She looked at me, as if she was asking for my approval for being saintly, and thought she wasn't going to get it. Well, she was dead right there! He *shouldn't* have been walking dogs on the mountain with his chest problem, but then nobody asked him to. Nobody asked him to go for extra slices from the fancy cheese counter, either, but it hadn't stopped him!

'Mrs Walsh says he looks terribly failed,' she said.

'We're not so hot ourselves!' I said, for I saw no reason why he should be let off the hook, after what he'd done to us.

'You mustn't be so bitter about him, Frankie,' he said.

It just took my breath away! All the scenery about my Dad she'd put me through, calling him every rotten thing she could think of and now suddenly I was supposed to be sorry for him, and it wasn't really his fault that our household was up the chute!

'Well, you've changed your tune!' was all I could manage in the circumstances. I mean, nothing had changed, and the way things were going I was about to be left as the one Dad-hater, in a houseful of runaway-father-fans.

'It's just this thing, Frankie,' she said, tapping the letter.

'What thing?' I said, angrily.

Then I got it. She didn't like handing him over to the Welfare. I almost laughed out loud ... *informers*. Informing was what she was on about! In the circumstances it was an echo of the other problem ... the awful problem that I couldn't even tell her about, if I wanted to keep her with her feet on the deck! If she thought the Provos were after him as well we'd have a screaming match!

'It's a bit late for second thoughts about going to the Welfare now,' I said. 'You had to go. You'd no choice. It was the right thing to do.'

'Yes, well ... you will come with me, won't you?' she said. 'To the court. If I have to go to the court, like the letter says, you'll back me up?'

'Yes,' I said. 'Sure.'

'You don't mind?'

'It is the right thing to do,' I said, and I was thinking: like going to the cops about who-got-Bob-Allen would have been the right thing to do, only he hadn't done it ... probably hadn't done it. And what I still wanted to know was *would* he have done it, if he'd known something and there was no way I could know that.

'It just seems so final,' she said, as if she hadn't heard what I'd said. Maybe she hadn't. She was way back in *her* life, thinking what it meant for her, and for him, betraying all the things they'd done together, and meant to each other.

'*He's* responsible for what's happened, Mum,' I said. 'Not you.'

I heard myself say it, sounding so angry, and I didn't even know if it was true.

I didn't hate him.

I love him.

I just don't know how somebody could walk out on another person like that, when they've been together for donkey's years having kids and watching them grow up and getting the things for a house and living in it and having fights and suddenly *snap*! Off with the Cheese Lady!

I don't know how he could do that to her! It wasn't as if she was awful, or anything. They were just like anybody's Mum and Dad. He gave her things, now and then, wee

62

surprises. And I suppose she yapped at him, and watched her old T.V. that drove him out of the room to his cross-word book in the kitchen. I mean, in some ways she is *stupid* ... but in others she is not. She used to yap at him when he lost the job ... and by the end she yapped at him a lot, and they hardly talked. The end of the yapping was that he stayed out, bad chest and all, and I suppose that that is how he took up with Mrs Evans, though how he found her on the cheese counter I don't know, for my Mum did all the shopping ... what shopping there was. She knew about it ... Mum, about him and Mrs Evans ... she knew for ages, and she never let on to me and Gerry. We didn't know about it until one Sunday it was Goodbye, and he wasn't there, and she was in her chair in front of 'Songs of Praise' looking absolutely small as if every bone in her body had shrunk. She must have been *so* certain of him, deep down, that she couldn't fathom it when he cleared out.

I couldn't forgive him that.

There was a *big scene* that Sunday.

Gerry stormed off upstairs, and I was left trying to hold the wobbly bits of Mum together, on the sofa.

The result was that Gerry ran off to the Walshs', leaving me stuck at home with my Mum while she *hated*. I didn't know she could be like that. I didn't know she could hate so much, and I couldn't cope with it.

Then I had to go with her to the Walshs', and watch the whole thing there, Gerry screaming, and Mrs Walsh trying to stop them.

In the end of it, I got Gerry out of the house to talk to her up among the plantation trees above the harbour.

I told her she would have to stop it. She couldn't stay at Mrs Walsh's, she would have to make her peace with

Mum and come back to Unity Close.

'I *can't*, Frankie,' she said.

I can still see her saying it. She was in her school uniform. She looks all right in it, most people don't. I never did. I looked a sight. The skirt is light green, with a blue blouse, and green cardigan. Her face was white, and her black hair came down around her. Her cheeks had shrunk in, so that her head looked like a skull, and her skin was dead too.

She came back. I worked on her, and Mrs Walsh worked on her, and we got an uneasy peace between her and Mum, but only just. Mum got her some clothes as a make-up present ... I think Mrs Walsh probably gave her the money ... and Gerry put the clothes on all right ... she *likes* clothes ... but she never gave Mum any thanks for them. It was as if they'd turned up in her wardrobe by magic. She started going out in them and living without us, and that made Mum mad too.

That was when I did my act, not sitting the exams.

The whole house fell apart.

That's what I blame him for ... for being the cause of it. I blame him, but it doesn't stop me loving him ... for I blame her too.

They were the *two* of them ... the *Raffertys* ... and then they weren't.

Why did they do it to us?

All that was going through my head, while Mum went on and on and on about having to go to court, and the letter, and how bad she felt about it and at that moment Gerry walked in, all glossy black hair and rosy cheeks, looking like something off a calendar, with her posh clothes and her green and purple school scarf up around her ears.

Her big nose was all red.

'Mum has to go to court, Gerry,' I told her. 'We've just had a letter.'

'He's made me do it, Geraldine,' Mum said.

She wasn't asking for Gerry's approval, as she had with me, she was telling Gerry what was what, and *daring* her to throw one of her scenes.

'You know your own business best,' Gerry said, sulkily.

'Our business,' Mum said.

'Count me out of it!' Gerry said.

'Hold on,' I said. 'Everybody take it easy! There is no point in having a row about it.'

'Nobody is!' said Mum.

'Unless *you* want to, Frankie?' Gerry said.

I could have thumped her!

After the day I had been through, with Con and Patrick and the *dirty* business about the shed wall and all the trouble I was in ... and *she* was being sweet reason.

Mum must have smelt the brimstone. 'Yes, calm down, Frankie,' she said.

'You take everything too personally, Frankie,' Gerry said.

'*Me!*' I said.

'Sit down, dear, and I'll make you a cup of tea,' Mum said.

I didn't even know I was standing up! I sat down, and she went into the kitchen to make it.

Then I got up.

'You all right, Frankie?' Gerry asked, anxiously.

I felt like saying sure I was. My Dad had run off, my house had gone mad, and the wee boys were painting things about me on shed doors, the sort of things that might lead to a knee-cap job.

'I'm just fine and dandy,' I said, and I went into the hall and got my coat and banged out of the house.

They could make what they liked of that!

Chapter 8

I just walked.

Walked and walked.

A part of me didn't know where I was going, and a part of me did ... but wouldn't admit *why*.

I got there, anyway.

The Moores' bungalow, out on the back road.

To see what had happened to Philip, that's the *why* I kept telling myself, because I was feeling guilty about Philip ... but of course that wasn't it, and I knew it wasn't.

Philip *knows* me. He would be someone to talk to.

So I went up and rang the doorbell ... and it wasn't a bell, it was chimes. They played 'Bless This House' or something.

And I was thinking: *What am I doing? I'm not supposed to be here, even!* At the end, with Philip, it had got to the point where we both agreed I wouldn't go to his house, because my existence was red-rag-to-a-bull as far as his mother was concerned.

Well, there I was, waiting on the doorstep, while the house blessed itself in four chords.

Mrs M. came to the door.

'Philip?' I said.

Her face set.

'You know you're not welcome here,' she said, straight out, no beating about the bush.

'That's for Philip to say,' I said.

'Philip doesn't wish to see you,' she said.

'I want to hear him say it,' I said. 'Not you.'

'Please, go away,' she said.

'You're a rotten old bitch!' I said.

She slammed the door and I was lucky I got my nose out of the way!

I put my finger on the bell push and blessed-this-house, ding-dong-ding, ding-dong-ding, ding-dong-ding. She was in the hall. I could see her shape through the frosty glass.

'I want Philip!' I bawled at her.

'Go away!' she shouted back.

'I'll kick your door in!' I shouted.

'If you don't go away, I'm calling the police!' she shouted back.

'Call the bloody cops then!'

She *did*.

I heard the telephone ting as she lifted it, and she started to dial.

'PHILIP!' I shouted.

He didn't come.

She was talking on the telephone.

Hell!

I went down their drive. They have a big house. It is called 'Arcadia'. They had a burnty-wood sign hanging from a post.

I hunched up and went back down the hill, towards town, wondering if a cop car would be on its way to pick me up and finish my day for me, but no cop car came. Maybe she hadn't called the police after all. She was only faking it, to get me off the front lawn.

I felt ... I don't know what I felt. Stupid. Mad. *Dirty*. I'd done everything wrong.

68

It was a long walk back from Philip's to our house. I had plenty of time to think about it. Back through the town, and up past the factory wall.

There was a new bit of graffiti on it.

I stood there looking at it.

It wasn't very big letters, and it was down at the side, so maybe not many would see it. Maybe Mum wouldn't.

I got a bit of mud, and smeared it. The mud was dead cold, because of the slush that was over it.

My hand hurt, with the cold.

For a moment I thought I would turn round on my heel and go to McCluskeys' and tell him straight what I thought of him, Con and his army of hangers-on, with their white paint, writing things on walls. But I couldn't even do that, because he mightn't know about it ... Con doesn't *order* things like that.

It was a wee boy did that. A Harty, or a Curly, one of the dirty little hang-on-the-corner-boys.

In the end, I didn't do anything.

I just went home.

Nobody said anything particular to me when I got in. My Mum and Gerry must have decided to gloss over it, as if I had never marched out on them.

We had a cup of tea, presided over by the letter behind the clock, which was peering at me out of the jagged tear at the top of the envelope, with 'Department of Health and Social Services' on it.

I went up to bed.

Ten minutes later, Gerry came up after me. She closed the door carefully behind her, and leant against it.

'Well?' she said.

I was lying humped up in bed, over on my side. I didn't say anything to her. I didn't think there was anything that needed saying, not to *her*. She wasn't on my side.

'Is it Dad you're upset about?' she said.

'No,' I said.

She sat down on the end of the bed, and patted my foot through the blankets. I pulled my foot away.

'He's upset about you,' she said.

I just *hmmm*-ed.

'*You* hurt him,' she said.

'*He* hurt me,' I mumbled.

'You shouldn't have yelled at him in the street,' she said. 'You should have let him in, at least. It's *his* house.'

'It's *my* house,' I said.

How come she knew about Dad coming to the house? How come I was to blame for everything?

'I didn't shout at him,' I said. 'I just told him where he could go.'

I wasn't shouting at him, anyway. At least I don't think I was. Maybe I was. There seemed to be a new me about, a me who bawled people out in the street, and went playing doorchimes, and shouting through letterboxes at women I didn't like, and got her name written up on factory walls.

I was all confused.

'He wants you to go and see him,' she said.

'I'm not going to see him, ever!' I said.

'It's not all one-sided, the way you think it is,' she said. 'And there's Daisy.'

Daisy? Daisy must be his cheese counter lady, Mrs Evans. Gerry would know that, because she had been seeing him ... betraying us, me and Mum, all caught in the mess Dad and his Daisy had left behind him.

'You've got to stop blowing your top, Frankie,' she said. 'I can't even talk to you any more. You know I can't.

Nobody can. Not Mum, even. You're ... you're acting hysterical, all the way.'

'That's a big laugh,' I said. 'Coming from you!'

'I *want* to *talk* to you,' she said. 'I want to help.'

'I don't want your help.'

'What do you want, then?' she asked, impatiently. I wasn't looking at her ... well, I was, but not directly. I was watching her in the mirror, where she couldn't see. I had my back to her, lying in bed, but I could see her and she didn't know. It was a kind of triumph.

She sat there on the end of the bed, with her hand just beside the bump of my foot. She didn't try to touch it again.

She's really *beautiful*, our Geraldine. I found myself thinking she might grow up to be a film star or something. Big grey eyes, fine skin, and dark, glossy hair that floats around her, and an easy way of moving in her clothes, as though they're not *on* her, she belongs in them. I wish I could wear clothes like that ... but then I don't, because that would be wishing away my disaster coat, which is a sort of second skin. I bought it at a jumble sale, a second skin to live in ... or *hide* in, I suppose.

'*You* were the sensible one,' she said. 'When I was having *my* hysterics at Mrs Walsh's house, you were the one who got me through it. And you never gave out at Mum. So what has happened now?'

Long pause.

'You've flipped your lid, or something!' she said, impatiently.

I never said a word.

'Well, look, if you want to talk, I'm here. Okay?'

'I don't want to talk to you,' I said.

'You've said that,' she said.

'Leave me alone,' I said.

'I can't help if you won't let me,' she said.

I let her stew on that. I wasn't going to give her the satisfaction of crawling to her, when all the time she was in with my Dad, and his Daisy. Daisy! What a name for a Fancy Woman!

'In the circumstances, I think I'd better go!' she said, and went to the door.

'Goodnight, Frankie?' she said.

'Get stuffed,' I said.

'Charming!' she said, and she went out.

My *beautiful* sister.

Chapter 9

I was up early.

I didn't even make myself a cup of coffee or anything, because I didn't want to wake them, and have them chasing down the stairs to see what I was doing.

I stuck an apple in my pocket and put my coat on and headed out of the house, for a walk, all by myself to see if I could sort things out.

I went down to the town, and along the Sea Road to the Promenade, straight down by the Ladies Lavatory, out onto the beach.

It wasn't as cold as I thought it might be. There was a weak attempt at sun, though the street lights were still burning.

I got onto the dry sand, for my walk.

The dry sand has a terrible way of getting into your toes, so I changed my mind and got off it. I went out and out and out across the wet sand, right to the lip of the tide, where I turned back and had a look at the town.

The mountains are very big. They were framed against the dark sky. The town was a ribbon coiled around their feet ... mountains don't have feet, but you know what I mean. If they were buried prehistoric monsters, all covered in soil, maybe they would have feet ... then, if they stirred and slipped forward just a bit, the whole town would be gone. Anyway, they're not going to move. Mountains don't move. They just crush you by being there.

I was summarising things in my mind, or trying to. I walked along the edge of the tide munching my apple. One of the waves rippled round my feet. It was too quick for me, and I got wet feet.

Cold feet.

Well, I had cold feet both ways.

Feet are funny, if you think about them. Any situation you find yourself in, *any* situation, your feet can carry you out of. All you have to do is to turn them round and keep walking.

I could do that. I could keep walking till I got to the Stranraer boat, and take the boat, and then take the train down to my Auntie's in Braintree, which is outside London somewhere, in Essex. I like my Auntie. She has no kids. I could move in to her house and live there.

People would say that was running away, ducking out of responsibilities.

I think that sometimes running away is the thing to do, if you know you can't manage. Everybody says to you, 'You mustn't run away. You must learn to face up to things.' But that doesn't mean that everybody is right. Mostly they are, but not all the time. It is a matter of fine judgement. Coping with the uncopable-with only lets you in for disaster! I thought maybe I was growing up at last, that I could think of a thing like that ... just walking out on the whole scene, and *not* feeling I was running away ... because I *wasn't*. I was facing up to the fact that I couldn't cope and saying well, why *should* I try to cope, when it can't be coped with?

So I could go to my Auntie Agnes in Braintree and if anybody said I was running away I would just say they were off their noddles, because all I was doing was doing what they tell you to do ... going looking for a fresh start, somewhere where I could get a job, which I wasn't going to get at home.

Home.

Ballybeg is a grand place to live, if it wasn't such a hole. There's the mountains, and the sea, and the Prom, and the row of grey Victorian houses on the Harbour Road, and the R.U.C. station with its high wire fortifications to keep the bombers out, and there's the old Cistercian Abbey at the back with the Holy Well. There are six dingy trains a day to take you out of it, and an odd bus, the Fortwilliam one, and the one to Killoo, along the coast. They go past Feney's Bridge, and Dunphy's Hole. This guy Dunphy threw his Dad down a hole in the cliff top, and tried to make off with the profits. It's an *idea*, but my Dad has no profits to make off with. I wouldn't fancy making off with his Daisy or a greyhound, and that is about all my Dad has going for him, these days. Any road, Dunphy got himself caught, and hanged!

I didn't want to leave, because it's my place.

I didn't want to let *them* make me leave ... all the *thems*, my Mum and Dad, and the nuns at school who said I was a washout for not doing their exams, and Philip's rotten mother, and the little kids who were writing things about me on the walls ... I still couldn't *understand* the thing about the writing on the wall.

I came up on the road by the bridge, where the talking parrot is—the parrot outside Rudi's. Rudi must have packed his parrot away, overnight.

I made up my mind *not* to make up my mind.

It *was* running away, and I'm not the running away sort.

I made up my mind I would stick it out and I would see

what happened and the other thing I was going to do was I was going to see my Dad.

I was going to see my Dad to try to sort it out with him, and when I'd done that then maybe I would run away, if he said that was what I should do. I'd ask him anyway, but I wasn't going to rely on him.

I wasn't going to take his word for anything, I just wanted to know what he'd think about it. And anyway, I couldn't go away without seeing him, because it was too important.

It would be a big bit of my life left unresolved if I went and never saw him again, because he might die with his chest and everything.

He had such big plans for me once, and he really tried to make them work. He used to help with my homework, when I was little, and he even pretended to help later on, when the homework I was doing was too much for him. He'd look at what I was doing, writing an essay or something, and he'd make suggestions. Often they were silly suggestions, but I didn't mind. It was his way of trying to keep in touch with me. And I'd do the same. I sat with him in the kitchen and helped out with his crossword puzzles, and when we got something right he was dead pleased, and he'd go on and on and on about it.

I used to like our nights in the kitchen.

Maybe they were part of the trouble, for my Mum. We didn't sit in with her, she was cut-out in front of her T.V. set, and that was her own fault, because she could have switched the thing off, and we'd have come in and been together, like we used to be ... why wasn't he *together* with her? What went wrong between them? I ended up saying to him that we should count Mum in more, but he couldn't do it, and in the end I tried to do it myself, and I took

Mum's side in things ... at first to try and get them together, and then because I felt it must be his fault, because he was smarter than she was, and he should have been able to stop what was happening. All that did was to cut me off from Dad. Gerry became *his* girl, and I was Mum's, that was the way it looked to everybody, but I think that he loved me more than Gerry, because he must have known I loved him in a way she didn't. She was always showy about it, but I loved my Dad a quiet way, and he loved me the same way, even when we were on different sides in the rows ... he must have loved me. He wouldn't have been crying when I shouted at him in his old greyhound van if he hadn't loved me, would he?

That's where I'd got to, when the police car came down the street.

It pulled up in front of the bank, and I came walking up towards it.

A cop got out of the car.

It was my cop that had been down at the Buildings—the one I'd decided was a human being.

He stood there waiting for me to go past him.

'Miss Rafferty?' he said.

'Yes,' I said.

I never blinked at him.

What did he think I was up to? Did he think I was out to rob the bank?

'I was looking for a word with you, Miss Rafferty,' he said.

I took that in.

I didn't particularly *want* to be seen with a cop, in the middle of the street, but there was no help for it.

'We've had a complaint about you, Miss Rafferty,' he said. 'Harassment!'

'What?' I said. Then I got it. Mrs Moore.

'Do you know what I'm talking about?' he said.

'Yes,' I said.

'We can't have the likes of you turning up on door-steps disturbing people,' he said. 'Do you understand?'

'Yes,' I said.

'This is by way of a friendly warning,' he said. 'Any more of that behaviour, and you could find yourself in trouble.'

'I suppose so,' I said.

'Leave your boyfriend be!' he said, and he grinned in through the door of the car at his mate.

'Philip Moore isn't my boyfriend,' I said.

'Good,' he said.

'Can I go now?' I said.

'Nobody is stopping you,' he said.

So I went.

I was *embarrassed*. It was worse than that. The word would be all over the place that I'd been up to the Moores' house after Philip, and his mother had called the cops on me. I didn't know where to put myself.

My face was burning, walking away down the road from the cop car trying not to look at people.

It was *mortifying*.

I could cheerfully have taken Mrs Moore and hung, drawn and quartered her for doing a silly thing like calling the cops when all it was was a wee row ... well, I suppose I did lose my temper and shout a few things at her, but she should have known better. I would have gone straight up to Phil's house and told her what I thought of her—only of course that was just what I couldn't do, for fear of getting my name in the papers.

I never felt so humiliated in my whole life.

I don't know how I got back to our house, but I did, and then I had to put a brave face on it because my Mum and Gerry were up and walking round the house, and very discreetly not asking the patient where she'd been.

I'd *die* if the word got back to them!

The main thing it did was to steady in my mind the idea about going away, and *that* steadied in my mind the other idea.

I was going to see my Dad.

Chapter 10

I was in the middle of thinking about that, and figuring *how* I was going to see my Dad, how I was going to set about doing it, I mean, when there was a stupid intervention.

Skyscraper Calvert turned up at the door, with a message that Mr Leyland wanted to see me down at the Tech.

'Oh, glory!' I said. 'Was he mad?' Maybe he had heard tales about me and the Moores, and he was having me in for a lecture, and then I thought it couldn't be that, because that was private and personal and none of his business, even if I did get myself arrested.

I was going to tell Skyscraper to clear off and tell Mr Leyland I wasn't coming, and then I thought better of it, because it was time to get myself back on the rails.

I got on me and left.

Skyscraper was loitering beside the painted gable, waiting for me.

He had his bike with him ... or somebody's bike that he'd borrowed. I don't think he could afford a bike like that, with shiny pedals and gears. He wheeled it down the road beside me and kept nattering.

We must have looked really dumb. He is about 6' 3" and I am about 5' 6" ... not dumpy, but not very big.

'We're like Laurel and Hardy,' I told him.

'The long and the short of it!' he said. It wasn't great

repartee, but it was an improvement on the late, great Philip Moore, and his Mammy.

'You didn't see Phil about, did you?' I asked, awkwardly, because I was going to have to face up to Philip before I went away and explain about the scene with his mother. I owed him that much.

'Philip's away,' he said, sounding surprised. 'Didn't you know?'

I gaped at him.

'Away?' I said.

'He had a row with a parrot!' Skyscraper said. 'Were you not in on it?'

'No,' I said.

'You're not still going out with him, then?' Skyscraper said.

'Evidently not!' I said.

'Uhuh!' he said, looking pleased.

'So tell me about the parrot,' I said, trying to sound as if it really didn't matter.

'Phil smashed the parrot,' Skyscraper said.

'What parrot?' I said.

'Rudi's parrot,' he said. 'Your Phil was sozzled, and he put his boot through the parrot, and Winston caught him and dragged him up to the Moores' house in the car and Darky Moore near whaled the life out of him, and the upshot of it was that Darky put it down to bad company, and he keel-hauled Philip out of town to I don't know where, but somewhere where there are no parrots to kick in!'

I let it sink in. Bad company!

No wonder Mrs Moore had the cops on me! She must have blamed me for Rudi's parrot, as well as everything else ... Rudi's *late* parrot, that is!

'So it is bye-bye Phil,' he said, and there was something in the way he looked at me which made me sense the way his mind was going.

Well, I wasn't going with it!

'I'm off men,' I said, quickly.

'But not for the duration,' he said, hopefully, looking down fondly at the top of my skull. I felt really silly with him up there and me down here. I could never go out with anybody as tall as that. It must be a real handicap for poor Skyscraper. He wouldn't want to go out with me anyway, if he knew the whole story!

We came up by the Tech. It is called Ballybeg College of Further Education, but really it is the old Tech, with a new name stuck on it, and the Truck in charge. I mean Mr Leyland. We call him the Truck because of Leyland Trucks, and also because he goes around all day hooting at people, and with his glasses off half the time he doesn't see where he is going. He's likely to run you down overtaking in the corridor. Since the Truck took over they've built on a new gym, round the back where there used to be a field, and they've also expanded into the chipboard factory, where my Dad used to work, and they've put Portacabins in the loading bay where the lorries used to pick up the chipboard, when there was chipboard to pick up. They're in the business of making us all think we are going places with Industrial Training, and pretending there is somewhere for us to go ... but I'll say this for the Truck, he tries.

I went into the Tech, down the corridor, and knocked at the Staff Room door. I could see that his room was empty, so I knew he wasn't in it, and there didn't seem to be anyone else about. The teachers were all on holiday, like everybody else, hanging around waiting for their Christmas credit-carding to catch up on them.

It is well for them that they have credit cards. I'm getting mine when I take the Bluebird up to heaven, if God hasn't changed the rules by then. Probably he'll have upped the admission so it is Angels only.

My Dad never even sent us a Christmas card. I don't know why that came into my head ... but it was in it, as I knocked the door. Maybe it was the Christmas cards pinned on the notice board outside the Staff Room.

You'd think he could have managed a Christmas card.

Miss Leonard opened the door. She's a fierce one, our Free Presbyterian follower of Ian Paisley, for God and Ulster and the Rope ... she Knows What Is Right, and that frightens me, because in Free Presbyterian eyes what is wrong *is* wrong, and if you're wrong you are the devil's child, and you've had it. She takes off every Election Day and rides around the country in her car with Union Jacks on the bumpers, and half a dozen voters in the back seat, admiring the pictures of Paisley on her sun flaps.

She doesn't like me. That's not sectarian, just ordinary not-like. I don't really blame her!

'Hullo, Frances,' she said, all pally, now-we're-out-of-term-we-can-relax-things-a-bit pally.

Nobody else calls me Frances.

'Mr Leyland wants to see me,' I said. 'He sent Bob Calvert down with a message.'

'Jack?' she said, over her shoulder.

'Come in, Frankie!' the Truck's voice boomed from the background. He's Official Unionist, which is to say ordinary Protestant, not Kick-the-Pope, like Miss Leonard. I'm not exactly saying he'd take to the Pope, if the Pope turned up in his garden, but he'd pass the time of day and be polite before showing His Holiness the road to the border.

The Truck was down on his knees, trying to screw

together the panels at the back of the filing cabinet. All that class of stuff is collapsing at the Tech, because of the cuts. He wasn't making much of a hand of it, to judge by the vein in the centre of his forehead, which was bulging. He has wispy red hair, and it falls down over his face, though not as far as his glasses. He doesn't clean his glasses well enough. They're always sort of smeared. I don't know how he sees out of them.

'What did you want to see me about, Mr Leyland?' I said.

'Mrs Walsh was in to see me about you,' he said.

'Oh,' I said.

Eileen Walsh interfering again. I didn't know she even knew him. Probably they booze together at the golf club, despite their politics. At *their* level, it is that sort of town.

'On her advice, I had a word with Sister Attracta at the Convent School.'

Attracta? She was our headmistress. What was he ringing the Convent School for?

'Father Quigley came in with Mrs Walsh,' he said. 'He's a man I have some respect for. He backed what she had to say.'

I didn't know what he was on about. Sister ... and Father Quigley? Father Quigley is the Curate. He was out at our house a lot when my Mum blew her gasket.

'Everybody seems to be of the same mind about you, Frankie,' he said. 'You're heading off the rails, and you need a second chance!'

'Oh,' I said, sounding and feeling not very pleased. I didn't want any favours from any of them. Especially Sister. She was really mad at me when I didn't do her old exams.

'The suggestion is that you are wasting your time in Miss Leonard's Business Studies, and that we ought to

switch you back to where you ought to be ... A Levels!'
he said.

'No,' I said.

'You might like to think a bit before you answer,' he
said, looking up at me from the floor, where he was still
crouched, holding the filing cabinet screws.

'No,' I said. 'I think I'm probably going away from here
anyway, and I don't want to be involved.'

'Away?' he said.

'I might be,' I said.

He frowned.

'Have you a job to go to?'

I shook my head.

'I thought not. Then take my advice ... *our* advice, for
we're all trying to help you ... get something behind you
first—then go.'

'I'm going when I want to,' I said. 'I'm not bothered
about A Levels.'

'Miss Leonard says you aren't bothered about your work
for her, either,' he said, suddenly irritated. 'So what are you
bothered about?'

'I'm sorry if I get on her nerves,' I said. She was probably
worried about her results. She kept saying I would fail the
Business Studies if I didn't pay attention but I knew I
couldn't fail, because her course was for dodos!

'I'll pass her exam,' I said, thinking: *I will if I'm here to sit
it*, but not saying it, because I didn't want to emphasise
the going-away idea. I was annoyed at myself for letting
it slip out casually like that, but he had wrong-footed me.
He would tell Mrs Walsh what I'd said, and she would go
round to my Mum and there would be ructions. I con-
sidered asking him not to tell anybody, but I didn't. He
would only think that I was running away.

Well, I was.

If I went, I was, but I didn't know if I was going, not for certain. I still had to talk to my Dad first, in case something he said would make things seem different.

'I know what I want to do with myself, Mr Leyland,' I said, and I left him hunting his screws round the floor. He'd dropped some.

I went out the back way, past the fire station, partly to evade Skyscraper, because I was in no mood to go courting with a beanpole who thought his big chance had come, and partly because I wanted to go down by the river, where I used to go with my Dad.

My Dad was really great, then. He used to take me along the riverbank at weekends, when he wasn't working. Me and Gerry, that is. And he'd talk to us, and walk with us, and we'd look to see if the swans had their nest made, and he would tell us what great girls we were going to be, and all the opportunities we had coming. That's when we were in Primary School, and everybody was saying we were smart. He told us we would end up in university, and you could see he was so proud of us, all bucked up inside. He told us stories too, I know he made them up ... because we were in the stories. We'd sit down by the riverbank and he'd talk and talk and Gerry and I thought he was the best Dad in the world, and better than any other Dad that ever was.

I got down to the bridge, but I didn't go along the riverbank.

He wasn't going to be there, waiting for me.

The good of it had gone. I turned down the road, wondering what things had come to. Imagine priests and nuns and Free Presbyterians, the whole bang issue of them, all ringing each other and patting each other on the head and telling each other what Good Christians they were for spotting me making a mess of my golden opportunities.

I went down onto Hamilton Road, which leads up to the crossing our road leads into, and turned down it.

Then I knew I'd made a mistake.

The cops were there, and the army.

There was a car half way through the hedge, in someone's front garden, and the cops were stringing tapes across the road.

Sam Harvey the breadman was there.

'What happened?' I asked him.

'Some fella got shot,' he said.

'Was it the Provos?' I said.

'No,' he said. 'Army.'

'Oh,' I said.

'The car's all riddled with bullets,' he said. 'There's two fellas in it.'

'Where's the ambulance?' I said.

'Those fellas have no call for an ambulance,' he said.

It was awful the way he said it. He said it with a sort of satisfaction. He was *pleased*.

I moved away from him.

There was glass all over the road. The car must have skidded off it, and gone straight through the hedge of the house. I didn't know whose hedge it was. The car was stuck there, half in the garden and half in the pavement, and the doors were hanging open as if somebody had yanked them hard.

I could see a sort of dark shape, down by the side of the door, half out of the car.

A cop came up and talked to Sam, then Sam turned his bread van round, a neat three point turn, and drove back up Hamilton Road.

There were a whole lot of people gawking.

I was no better than they were.

I was gawking too.

A cop came up to the white tape that was across the road in front of us.

'Move along now,' he said. 'There's nothing here to look at.'

Everybody eddied back, but nobody moved, except a wee woman, Mrs Brady from the baby shop on the front. She wanted to get through to her car. It was parked at the other side.

'Nobody's getting through here, Mrs Brady!' the cop said.

'But you know me,' she said.

'If the Secretary of State knew you, it wouldn't get you through here!' the cop said.

Then a young fella spoke to the cop.

'That's one back for Bob Allen!' he said.

'Two-one to us!' the cop said.

Then another cop, an older one, came up and started giving orders to the crowd to move.

I went.

I was feeling sick inside.

Two-one, like a football match.

There were two men dead in the car.

Men maybe with wives and children and old grannies that had looked after them, riddled full of bullets just like that, for being in the wrong place, at the wrong time.

Only it wouldn't be like that.

Not if it was the army.

If it was the army, they'd either driven through a road-block, or it would be an ambush of some kind. Two Provos on their way in a car, and the army had got them.

I hoofed it home the back way, in time for the news bulletin, so I could find out what was going on. The other end of Hamilton Road was blocked off at the crossing in front of Church Lane. There were two police tenders there, and the same old white tape.

My Mum was making tea when I got in.

She hadn't heard a word about it.

She put the kettle off, and we turned on the Northern Ireland News, but there was nothing on it right up until the end, when they said something about reports coming in of an incident involving an army patrol in the town. A car had been fired on by the army, and it was believed there were casualties.

No names.

'Do you think there'll be trouble?' I asked my Mum.

'Of course there'll be trouble!' she said, and she added, 'Dear God help us if it is anyone from round here!'

Chapter 11

It was Patrick Hagen who came over and told us who they were.

He had a message from his Mammy, in the hospital. She wanted Mum to get some things for her.

'Lady's things,' Patrick said, awkwardly. 'She said if you'd ring this number and ask for Sister, the nurses would get her to the phone.'

I looked at my Mum.

I couldn't make out what Mrs Hagen would be wanting in the way of lady's things that a hospital couldn't lay on for her.

My Mum took the bit of paper with the number on it, and put it behind the clock. Then she said to Patrick: 'Who was it got shot?'

'Nobody from round here,' Patrick said. 'Two guys from Belfast.'

'Oh,' said my Mum.

She was thinking what I was thinking. If it was Belfast ones there maybe wouldn't be so much bother.

'There'll be a carry on,' Patrick said.

'What sort of carry on?'

'The Hartys and that lot are going up the Police Barracks,' Patrick said. 'The usual thing.'

'You steer clear of that, Patrick,' my Mum said. 'You

wouldn't want to be worrying your mother, and her in hospital.'

I was thinking that Mrs Hagen would have been one of the ones out organising the lot that were going up to the Police Station, but Patrick isn't like her—that's his problem, because being the odd Hagen out doesn't go down well with the natives. I didn't say a word. It was awkward, with Patrick standing there.

Patrick didn't say anything either.

Maybe he didn't think he was on safe territory.

My Mum started telling him all about his Ma's leg. She had told him it already, for she went over to the Hagens' house when she came back from the hospital, before she ever came near us. She'd come back full of orders for Daddy Hagen's dinner!

They nattered on.

I sat there, thinking about the dead men in the car with the bullet holes in it. I felt really *sick* inside. I didn't want to be part of all the fuss there'd be ... the protest and the lamentations. I was going to have to tell Mum what I felt some time, and that meant telling her that I was thinking of going to my Auntie's in England, if I could.

I didn't know what way she would take it, and I wanted to have her on my own before I would say it.

In the end, Patrick went.

He didn't say anything to me when he was going.

He kind of avoided my eye.

My Mum kept on talking, old nonsense about Mrs Hagen and the hospital. I looked at her and I thought in a minute I'll say it, but the minute didn't come ... maybe she sensed what I was going to say. She didn't talk about the dead men, although it was the obvious thing to talk about. If she had it would have given me my opening, and she wasn't going to do that. She wasn't going to make it easy for me. She kept on about Daddy Hagen. Apparently he had got word about Mrs Hagen somehow, out with his Beach Club, and he'd caught the bus into Fortwilliam and turned up at the hospital tight as a tick. Then he started trying to give orders to the nurses, and Mrs Hagen, who was sitting there with her leg all in plaster, let into him. In the end the porters got him out, and he headed for the pub down the hill. My Mum said she was glad to see the back of him, for she'd been dreading having to sit with him on the bus. Whatever happened to him, he never made the bus. Apparently he came back in the cab of Quilty's coal lorry, clutching a bunch of flowers he'd meant for Mrs Hagen, but hadn't handed them over because he never got the chance, with him shouting at the nurses and Mrs Hagen shouting at him. My mum said she went and hid in the Out-patients, down the corridor, till he was off the scene.

She won. I didn't tell her what she didn't want to know.

I went back to thinking about the two dead men from Belfast in the car, and how the dark thing I'd seen lying out of the front seat was probably one of them, only I was too far away to see it.

My Mum got herself settled down with her afternoon programmes.

I watched them with her, thinking maybe I wouldn't be able to do that much longer, if I went away to England, and wondering how she could cope without me, and if she could cope, and thinking really it was up to her to cope, for it was her own life and she had to lie on the bed she'd made for herself.

I had a life too to look after, and it was my own.

Then I went down the road for some bread.

Teresa Harty was coming up it, all on her own. I couldn't

understand that, because I thought she would be down at the Police Barracks, shouting things about the cops, and getting herself on the T.V. news saying the cops and the army were murderers.

Maybe they *were*.

Maybe the two guys in the car were just two guys in a car. All sorts of things can happen. Like it might be mistaken identity, or some army one going mad with his gun. Some are just baby soldiers, who wouldn't know any better. If it was that, then there would be a cover-up story, and the crowd would all be out shouting about it, and there'd be more fuss, and more writing on the walls.

Teresa Harty was on the other side of the road, but she must have seen me coming, because she crossed over and came up towards me and I nerved myself, because I didn't know what she was going to say.

She is one of them was the thought in my head. She was always a rebel, even when we were in school. She never put up with what the nuns told her if she didn't think it right. She was always going round making a name for herself.

She came straight on at me, up the pavement.

'Hi, Teresa,' I said.

She spat in my face.

Nobody ever did that to me before.

I was so taken aback that I froze.

She didn't say a word.

She went on past me. She didn't even turn her head to see what I'd do.

I went all shaky inside. I didn't shout, or run after her to pull her by the hair, what there was of it, or any of the other things you'd think I might have done.

I got my hanky out, and cleaned her spit off.

It was on my coat too, spoiling it.

I felt dirty.

I went on to the shops, putting my feet one in front of the other ... *my feet that were going to take me away out of it*.

I didn't make it to the shops.

My feet turned round on me.

I was thinking: *It's all down to Con McCluskey* and I was so mad I just couldn't let it go, and run away like that, without telling him it was all down to him, and the likes of him.

There was Bob Allen, trapped with his useless legs in his chair, and scores of others like him, both sides. And the two that were bullet-riddled in the car, them as well ... it was the likes of Con put them up to whatever *they* were at, when the army shot them. They were dead now, and somewhere there'd be somebody like my Mum, watching her Brookside or Coronation Street, who'd suddenly find herself with a hearse at the door, and the action coming home to her, off the T.V. screen. There'd be mums and dads and sisters and cousins, all bathed in blood, and there'd be Con sailing on, sucking his pipe and spouting his words about the Revolution and the day that was coming ... *Tiocfaidh ár lá*, the bloody day, when the Martyrs would march into their own.

I wanted to tell him what I thought of him, just the once, before my feet took me out for good.

The McCluskeys' house is down the end of the Estate. It is a neat little house in the middle of the row well kept and tended, with blue curtains and a blue door, very decent.

I went up the path and knocked the knocker.

Mrs McCluskey's sister Oona opened the door.

I know her, but she doesn't know me. I won a medal at

94

the Feis for Irish Conversation, and she was one of the judges. Her name is Oona McGivern, and she's married to one of the Fortwilliam McGiverns.

'Hullo, Mrs McGivern,' I said. 'I wanted to speak to Con.'

'He's not in,' she said. 'He's away up the Barracks.'

I should have expected that. He'd be on the march, handing in a letter of protest. Well, there was no way I was running up the street to pluck him out of a British Murderers Parade, where I might just not be the most popular person.

'Could I give him any message?' she said. She was red round the eyes, as if she had been crying. She must have noticed me noticing. 'I'm sorry,' she said. 'Everything's all bust up, you'll understand, with the trouble.'

'Yes,' I said.

'Bloody Brits!' she said.

'I know about it,' I said.

'Wee Sean,' she said. 'Wee Sean Corry, and Brendan Pearce!'

'Con's friend?' I said, the heart sinking inside me. All I could think of was the party, and this big drunken lad with the black hair mouthing slogans at me ... *that* Pearce, and now he was *dead*.

A real person *I knew*, dead.

'He'd no gun on him!' she said. 'Just riddled full of holes, the pair of them. Bloody murder, that's what it was, bloody murder.'

I opened my mouth to say something, and all that came out was an incantation. 'I'm sorry for your trouble.' And it didn't mean anything, not with that wee weepy woman on the doorstep in her cardigan, and with her red-rimmed eyes, and Pearce ... I didn't even want to think about

Pearce, because I couldn't bear the idea.

She stumbled, someway, against the door. She was dead white.

I put my arm round her and hugged her.

'The dirty murdering bastards!' she said.

'Yes,' I said. 'Yes.'

She wiped her eye with the back of her hand.

'Jesus God!' she said. 'The *bastards*!'

I had my hands on her, but I let them drop. I was trapped there in the awfulness of what was going through her, the bitter misery and hate.

'Bloody Murdering Bastard Brits!' she said, and the cursing seemed to stiffen her up for a minute.

'I'm sorry I disturbed you,' I said. 'I didn't know ... '

'Is there ... is there any message I can give him, when he gets back?' she said, meaning Con. She was taking a hold on herself, as best she could.

'Just tell him Frankie Rafferty called,' I said. 'Tell him I'm sorry, and all ... '

'Are you ... ?' she said.

'Yes,' I said.

And suddenly she was screaming and screaming and screaming at me.

Awful things.

Things I wouldn't say.

Things coming from right down inside her where the pain was.

She never touched me.

She just screamed and screamed after me.

And I ran away. What else could I do?

Chapter 12

It's got nothing to do with me.

That was the thought pounding in my head.

I was up our path and through the door and there was my Mum on her sofa and another face, a face I didn't want to see—Mrs Walsh.

Her wee car was outside.

I'd seen it, and not seen it, when I was running.

'Frankie . . .' my Mum said.

I was down on the sofa, up against her.

'God, Frankie, what happened?' she said.

And I told her.

I don't know what they made of it, my Mum and Mrs Walsh. It just poured out of me, all the wrong way round, about Teresa and Con and Oona McGivern screaming at me and Teresa spitting at me and the things on the wall . . . the whole lot. And Pearce. Big drunken Pearce with the dark curly hair, and the bullet holes in him.

'Oh God!' Mrs Walsh said.

'I'm scared,' I said.

'Of course you are,' my Mum said, and she was cradling me up against her. It was awful, and I was all in bits, but in a creepy way I remember feeling it was great, because she was just like *Mrs Rafferty* again, my Mum instead of the wrecked Mum I'd been looking after. The old one, the other Mum who looked after me, had come out from inside

97

the upset broken one that *I* looked after.

I cried and cried, up against her.

'We'll have to get you get out of this,' my Mum said.

I was wailing, I can remember that. No words. Just wailing.

'Poor Frankie,' Mrs Walsh said.

I wished that she wasn't there, but in a way I was too far gone to care.

'He'll have to cope with this!' my Mum said.

'Joe?' Mrs Walsh said.

My Mum shook me.

'Sit up, Frankie!' she said.

The wailing went on. I couldn't stop it. A kind of shiver was in me.

'Sit up!' my Mum snapped.

And I was up.

I had the cushion against me, and I was clinging onto that. I was *up*, with my head down and the wail inside me now, not out.

'I think you'd better go and see your Dad,' my Mum said.

I couldn't say anything.

'You'd *like* that, wouldn't you?' she said, gently. 'Eileen, would you...?'

'Put the coat on her,' Mrs Walsh said.

'You're very good, Eileen,' my Mum said.

Mum got my coat from the floor where I'd chucked it and she bundled it round me and then Mrs Walsh and Mum frog-marched me to the car.

'Get in,' my Mum said.

I got in.

'Are *you* coming?' Mrs Walsh said, to my Mum.

My Mum shook her head.

'What'll I say ...' I began.

'You're not to say I sent you,' my Mum said. 'Do you understand?'

'Yes,' I said.

'He's to get you out of this,' she said.

'I—'

'You're going out of this, Frankie,' she said.

'I *decide* if I go,' I said, rallying at the end, when it all seemed to be decided for me ... going to my Dad, going away ... I didn't like it. I wanted to decide things for myself. It wasn't like I was a little girl, and she and Dad had to look after me.

'You'd decided that already, Frankie,' my Mum said.

'But ...'

'You made your mind up about that, some time ago,' Mum said.

As the car turned off the Estate, the army were moving in.

'My God, Frankie,' Mrs Walsh said. 'What a day!'

Chapter 13

I don't think either of us spoke a word in the car after that, all the way to Fortwilliam, and then up a mountain road. Nobody decided it, or maybe Mrs Walsh did. Her face was all tight. I think she couldn't take any more.

It was all big things happening, and then it wasn't.

Just ordinary, in a car, except that it wasn't ordinary.

I was going to see my Dad.

We got to the foot of the lane where my Dad's house was, and that was as far as the car could go, without tank tracks. It was that sort of lane, leading up onto the mountain, in the middle of nowhere.

Mrs Walsh put the handbrake on, and sat there.

'Do you want me to come with you?' she asked, very carefully. The words came out of her almost one at a time. She didn't even look at me.

'No,' I said.

I absolutely definitely didn't, and I think she knew that, somehow. I'm sure she was relieved anyway. The lack of conversation in the car had got me back on my feet again. My own feet, not anybody else's, least of all hers. The odd thing was, she was helping me, and I didn't like her. I didn't want her interfering in my life.

I think she knew that. She might be a wee brandy-and-soda lady, but she had her head screwed on.

'You know the situation up there?' she said, grinding it out.

'Yes,' I said.

'You *do* though, don't you?' she said. 'I don't know how *much* you know ... how much they've been keeping from you?'

I let that sink in.

I wasn't sure what she was on about.

'Your Mum and Geraldine,' she said. 'They both thought, well ... you have been carrying on a bit, haven't you? I don't know how much they felt they ought to tell you?'

'How much about *what*?' I said.

'Your Dad and his ... *complications*,' she said, and I hated the primness of it.

'Daisy!' I said.

'Yes,' she said.

'I know the score,' I said.

'You're not to think too badly of your Dad,' she said, hurriedly. 'He did what he did ... well, there were all sorts of reasons.'

'My Mum was the reason,' I said. 'I know that.'

'Don't blame your poor mother ...' she began, but she didn't finish it.

I'd opened the door of the car. I got out.

She wound down her window.

'I'll wait for you,' she said. 'In case you need me.'

'I don't know how long I'll be,' I said.

'Your Dad might need me to help,' she said.

'You're very good, Mrs Walsh,' I said. Trying to make it sound polite and thankful, but really meaning *you're very good but I wish you'd go away*.

'It's no trouble, Frankie,' she said.

Then I had to ask her where the house was.

She might have told me, seeing she knew.

I didn't want to have to ask her.

I went up the lane.

It was getting dark over the mountain, snow was on the way.

I felt like somebody out of *Wuthering Heights*, only Cathy and Heathcliffe didn't have to cope with abandoned Dublin buses peering at them over a country hedge, like rusty cows. I read *Wuthering Heights* in Third Year. That's why I keep coming back to it.

Don't ask me what Dublin buses were doing halfway up the side of a mountain. Dublin is a border away, another country, but there they were, abandoned in the long grass on the field alongside the lane, with great hunks cut out of them for scrap.

It was cold, going up the lane, with the snow gathering in frozen ruts, and making the rocks that poked up out of it slippy.

I was on my way up the dark mountain, in the snow, with the bulk of it pressing down upon me. The cold was probably worse because I was on my way up from the sea. Ballybeg is down by the coast, so we don't get much snow, but up there on the high ground everything was freezy. The lane turned, and ran along beneath the foot of the mountain, edging up to the side.

What was I going to say to my Dad?

I hadn't a clue. What was I on my way up a bloody mountain lane in the snow for? To see a man about a dog? Only ... Mum said he'd have to get me out of it. That was the ticket. He'd have to get onto my Auntie Agnes in England and fix me up with somewhere to go where *they* couldn't get me ... but it wasn't fair, and it wasn't right and I didn't know *why* I had to be running away, when I hadn't done anything that was wrong, not to anybody.

Life isn't fair, was the thought, but it didn't take me very far.

Running up a lane ... *Daddy, Daddy, Daddy, help me!*

I should have *hated* that, because he'd broken me, that's what he'd done ... taken my life and smashed it apart with his Daisy, the-cheese-counter-lady ... but I was too far gone to fight it any more ... and anyway, if he had anything to give, any help at all ... didn't he owe it to me? I should have been too proud, and too strong, too much *me*, but there I was instead waiting for somebody to help me, making the admission that I couldn't help myself any more.

I should have hated it, but I was too mixed up, too hurt, too frightened.

That's all there was to it.

Somebody stronger might have done better, but I didn't.

The house wasn't much of a house ... my father's love-nest. It was made of tin, painted bright green, or what had once been bright green, but now the rust had got it, and the paint was dropping off, rippled by rust. There was a wire cage against one end, where the dogs my father walked must have lived, but there were no dogs there. It wasn't a proper dog run ... it was made of wire, tied on to old bed irons.

I banged the door.

It was a real *bang*. By this time my walk had put me in a door-banging mood.

A woman opened it.

She was in her late thirties, maybe, but built like a wee girl. Her feet were in sloppy slippers, and her hair was straggly.

'Are you Mrs Evans?' I said.

'Yes,' she said.

'Daisy?' I said.

She looked puzzled for a second, then she said: 'No.'

'Oh!' I said.

'The child's name is Daisy,' she said.

That's when I took in the baby.

I'd been thinking she was an odd shape, but she wasn't. There was this tiny bundle in her bird-bone arms, all wrapped in a bit of old blanket.

Daisy.

A baby ...

'You're ... you're ...?' she said.

'I'm Frankie,' I said. 'Is *that* his?'

It was terrible, calling her baby *that*. I asked the question *knowing* the answer, just straight out and hurtful ... *that* ... thinking nobody had told me or prepared me for this, and then thinking somebody had tried ... Mrs Walsh had tried, and Gerry had tried, after a fashion, and I'd not understood what they were saying to me, and they'd not understood that I didn't understand, with all the things that were happening around me. I had never thought of a baby.

So that was his reason.

Daisy. *That* had taken my Dad. *She*. She had taken my Dad from me, and now I'd never get him back. He'd been Daisy-chained!

The woman was frightened. I must have been one of her personal nightmares, coming at her out of the night, up the lane to the mountain, wild-eyed and wild-haired in my old disaster coat, banging at her door, as though I was going to smash everything.

She looked as if she would pass away on the spot. She was thin and pathetic, a birdy breed of a woman, with a

104

bony face and glasses and a pinny on her, all mucky. She had a hole in her tights, right below the knee and stretching to the shin ... the sort of hole you couldn't walk out with. Her sloppy slippers had been pink, but they were dirty grey now.

'I'm not going to hurt you,' I said. I had to say something. She was looking at me as if I was some snake or serpent, that would lash out my forked tongue and bite her, or some monster that would grab her baby and beat it against the wall ... and I wasn't. 'I didn't know there was a baby, that's all,' I said.

The woman worked her jaw, it was as if her face was about to fall apart, and I was doing it to her. I didn't want to hurt her, why would I?

It was his damn fault!

I was *supposed* to know about Daisy, and I didn't know. It was all a mix up in my head, that wouldn't go away because the realness of it was there in her arms, before me.

His baby.

My Dad's, that I didn't even know about. My half-sister!

'He never told me,' I said.

My half-sister gurgled at me.

'Hullo, Daisy,' I said, thinking she couldn't be as wee as I thought, if she could manage a gurgle. How long had she been about—how long had there been a Daisy, with nobody telling me?

'How old is she?' I said.

'Six weeks,' she said.

'Nobody told me,' I said, and I was thinking nobody told me because they thought I'd go up the wall but *somebody* had tried because I'd collected the name 'Daisy' somewhere along the line, only I thought it was her, the

Cheese Lady, and it wasn't, it was a baby.

Another me ... but it wasn't me. It had come out of *her*, not my Mum.

The Cheese Lady clutched it to her.

'Look,' I said. 'I'm not here for a fight, Mrs Evans. I have to see my Dad.'

'He's out,' she said.

'When will he be back?' I asked, thinking how stupid it sounded, like a formal visit. *She doesn't know what's going on* I thought, and the fierce thought that marched with it was *and she's not going to.* My mess was my mess, for me and my Dad, not for her ... not that she could have helped anyway. She was small and scared and defenceless and *old,* clutching her Daisy and waiting for me to let fly at her, or do whatever awful thing it was she thought I'd come to do.

'I *need* to talk to my Dad,' I said.

'I'll tell him you were asking,' she said.

Look, it's my Dad we're on about was the thought that welled inside me. *My Dad*, but she owned him now, and the baby owned him, and I had nothing at all.

It wasn't *fair.*

'You tell him I need him,' I said. 'Tell him he's got to come and help. Tell him I need him *now.*'

'We have no money, you know,' she said.

I could have hit her.

'I'm not looking for money,' I said.

Maybe I was. How was I going to get away without money? I was going to need money, but I'd get money some place. I needed him to be *my* Dad, not Daisy's.

The baby started to cry.

'Shush, ba,' she said, patting it.

'Will you tell him that? Tell him there's trouble. Tell him

I need to see him, quick. Will you? It's very urgent!'

She nodded.

You might ask me in, I thought, but I didn't say it. I couldn't have waited there with *her*, because I didn't like her and I didn't want her and I was too mixed up to trust myself not to say it, and do something that maybe couldn't be undone.

'Well, that's it then, Mrs Evans,' I said. 'Only tell him I need him now, like *right now*, like not tomorrow, okay?'

'Yes,' she said.

'That's all I have to say,' I said. 'I'm away home. I'll not disturb you and your child any longer.'

'It was lovely seeing you,' she said.

It was a daft thing to say, in the circumstances. I could barely credit it. I was probably the last person, barring my Mum or the Legal Officer from the Welfare, that she wanted to see.

''Bye, wee Daisy,' I said.

Mrs Evans humped the baby up in her arms.

'It's really urgent that I see my Dad,' I said. 'Tell him that. Tell him I've got to go to England, and he's got to help me, and that it's got to be *now*.'

I wasn't going to tell her why. That wasn't *her* business. I started to walk away.

'Mind yourself going down the hill in the dark,' she said, inanely as if she was talking to her Grannie.

I turned back and looked at her.

She might be pathetic inside, but that was no reason why she should get away with it. She'd bust up our home, and her own home with Mr Evans, and she was probably going to bust up her own baby's life as well, through being weak, and spineless, and letting people frighten her.

'You needn't bother telling him,' I said.

'But ...'

'I can look after my own self,' I said.

And I left her with it.

In a way, I felt *cleaned* inside. I could have said something to hurt her, or hurt him through her ... something like, *'you can tell my father that I have nothing to say to him, ever'*, but it wouldn't have been true.

The truth was that I wanted to do *it* ... whatever there was that I was going to do ... myself. Myself, alone ... me, myself, being myself, standing for myself, my own life. He wouldn't be out of it, he would never be that, but he wouldn't be *in* it, either, not the way he once had been. My Mum and Dad would just be two people I knew. They'd be in my past, *not* knowing me truly, ever again, because I'd be away from them, what they thought about me.

On my own from now on.

It didn't stop me crying, going down the lane.

The crying reinforced it.

I was still in a bad way when I got to the car.

'Get in,' Mrs Walsh said, in her clipped voice.

I got in.

'Well?' she said.

'He wasn't there,' I said.

'What do you want to do now?' she said.

'I want to go home,' I said.

'Is that wise?'

'No,' I said fiercely. 'It's not wise. But it is my home, and I'm going to it, and I'm getting my things and I'm clearing out of it and I'm not coming back. That's what I'm doing and I'm the one that has decided it and if you don't take me home I'll walk.'

She didn't look one bit pleased!

'I'm sorry, Mrs Walsh,' I said. 'But I'm all right now. I've sorted things out. I'll get some money somewhere and clear out. And I'll do it by myself.'

'I can give you some money for the fare,' she said.

'That's very decent,' I said. 'You'll get it back.'

So much for doing it all by myself!

'That's the least of my worries,' she said.

She put her hand in the dashboard and brought out an envelope with money in it. She handed it to me. She must have been getting it ready when I was up the hill.

She knew my Dad had no money.

She was very decent.

'You could come to the bungalow,' she tried, game to the last. Out to save me from me. 'I'd get Gerry to bring up your things. Or I could go down there and fetch them.'

'I want to go home, Mrs Walsh,' I said, firmly.

'You're either very brave, or very foolish,' she said.

'Yes,' I said.

'You don't deserve this happening to you,' she said, starting up the car. 'I wish I knew what to say to you, for the best.'

'I don't want to talk about it, Mrs Walsh,' I said.

'*Quite*,' she said, disapprovingly.

We sat there, driving back down the road to Ballybeg, where I wasn't going to *be*, any more.

I was all excited, all bucked inside, strong, *doing something*.

Nobody was going to smash me.

Chapter 14

The Estate was quiet when we got back to it. No sign of the cops, or rent-a-mob. I was surprised, remembering the number of soldiers there had been about the place when we left.

It was glowing orange from the street lamps, with the snow all mucked and dirty. Mrs Walsh had to go carefully, in case we skidded into anything.

She stopped outside our house.

'I don't think I'll come in, Frankie,' she said.

That was understandable! She looked dead nervy, afraid, I suppose, that the natives would emerge from the darkness outside the lamp glow and rip her bumpers off!

'You've been very good Mrs Walsh,' I said. 'I don't know how to thank you for all you've done and all you've put up with from me and my Mum and my family.'

It was my prepared speech. I'd been at it as we drove onto the Estate, in my mind. The result was that it came out stiff and wooden, composed, as if I didn't mean it, when I did. I meant it, but I still didn't like her. I couldn't help it. Body chemistry, I suppose.

'And also for the money,' I said, mad at myself for forgetting that. There must have been fifty or sixty pounds pounds in the envelope, neatly folded up.

'You'll get every penny back, as soon as I'm able,' I said.

'Don't worry about that, Frankie,' she said.

Then she told me I was to look after myself, and I wasn't to think too badly of my Mum and Dad or the neighbours, because if I started thinking like that it would poison my life.

I 'Yes-Mrs-Walsh-ed' her, and agreed with everything because I owed her that much, but really she didn't understand me at all.

'Things seem quiet enough here now,' she said. 'But you do know you'll *have* to go, don't you? Soon. Tomorrow, if you can.'

'Yes, Mrs Walsh,' I said. 'And thanks again, Mrs Walsh, for everything.'

Off she went.

Our door was bolted.

I had to ring the bell.

Gerry opened the door. 'Oh, it's you!' she said.

'Frankie!' my mother called.

I went into the front room. She was lying on the sofa, looking awful. The Belly Kelly was sitting in my Dad's chair. He had his hurley stick on the seat beside him.

'I didn't see him,' I said. 'I left a message.'

'Bloody typical!' my Mum said, sitting up.

The room was different. They had moved the chairs back, and taken down the ornaments. There were two buckets full of water by the window, and a basin full of sand.

'Oh, come on!' I said. 'This is ridiculous!'

'Come out here and take your coat off!' Gerry said, and she kind of pushed me back into the hall, and closed the door firmly behind her. She leant against it.

'What's going on?' I said.

'Con's friend Pearce was one of the men the army shot,' she said. 'He's dead. Con has been lifted by the cops. The

111

army say it was an ambush, and that Pearce had papers on him that implicate Con, but nobody believes it, because the story goes that they weren't operational. They were on their way here, and somebody tipped the army off, and it was an ambush. Pearce hadn't even a gun, so it was murder. It was on the T.V. and everything. All hell has been let loose.'

'Yes,' I said.

'There's a lot of talk about you, too,' she said.

'Yes,' I said.

'They say you've been talking to the cops,' she said. 'You know what *that* means, Frankie.'

My mother came out of the door.

'Frankie?' she said.

'Yes, Mum,' I said.

'It's not true, Frankie, is it?' my Mum said.

'No, Mum,' I said.

'You'll have to tell them it isn't true!' she said.

She was gone again. She knew, and I knew, that that just wasn't possible. They weren't going to believe anything I said.

'Go in and lie down, Mother!' Gerry said, sharply.

'Don't you give me orders, Miss!' my Mum snapped.

'She was seen with the cops this morning, Mum,' said Gerry. 'You can't deny that, can you, Frankie?'

'I never said a word to the cops!' I said.

'You were bloody *seen*,' she said, angrily.

'It wasn't like that,' I said, weakly.

'They're saying other things too, Frankie,' Gerry said. 'You and Patrick.'

'Patrick?' I said.

'You were seen carrying on with young Hagen in that room!' my Mum said, pointing at the sitting-room.

112

'ME? When?' I was too astonished to take it in. 'Me and Patrick Hagen?'

'The day I took his Mammy to the hospital,' my Mum said. She was quivery mad, now. I'd been thinking how she'd gone back to her *real* self, being the Mum who looked after me, but the real self had gone. She was working herself up for a big go at me.

'Patrick was never even in here,' I said, and then: 'Oh yes, he was, but only for a minute, getting the child.'

'The child being here only makes it worse!' my Mum said.

'*What* worse?' I said.

There was an awkward silence.

'Frankie, you were *seen*,' Gerry said. 'It's no good lying.'

'Seen?' I said. '*How* seen? Haven't we Venetian blinds on the front? Nobody can see in here.'

My Mum flapped her hands in the air, and then she started to cry.

I thrust past her into the sitting-room.

'Look!' I said. 'Bloody Venetian blinds!' Then I realised my mistake. 'There was nothing to see, anyway,' I said, but it sounded lame. I'd made it sound as if there was. 'Patrick came in here to collect the child, and we had a talk and he collected him, right?'

'You need your backside tanned!' my Mum said.

'Why don't you ask Patrick?' I said. *Patrick*. It would be him! The one Hagen who wasn't in the Supporters Club! 'This is all ... dead silly. I never did a thing. I never talked to the cops, I never carried on with anybody ...'

'Och, listen to yourself, Frankie!' said Gerry.

She didn't believe me.

Mum didn't believe me.

I was supposed to be carrying on with Patrick on our

113

sofa in front of the child, and I was supposed to be meeting up with the R.U.C. to give them information that got people shot and arrested and probably if somebody had said they'd seen me raping Santa Claus they'd have had me for that too.

'*Who* is saying all this?' I said. 'Does nobody believe me?'

'What anybody sitting in here believes makes no matter, daughter,' Old Belly said. He'd been sitting there like a stone man, hearing us yell at each other, making a spectacle of ourselves. 'It is what *they* believe out there that counts.'

'But that's where the stories are coming from!' I said. 'Teresa Harty and some of those ones, setting everybody against me.'

'Don't *screech* at us, Frankie!' Gerry said.

I *wasn't* screeching.

Maybe I was. I was all churned up. Nobody believed me. Nobody was going to help me.

'Well, why don't they come and petrol bomb us then?' I said. 'If everybody believes all this is down to me, why don't they come and do something about it?'

'I'm here to see that that doesn't happen,' Belly Kelly said.

I turned away from him.

'You believed me this afternoon, Mum,' I said. 'Why don't you trust me now?'

'I don't trust anyone any more,' she said bitterly. 'You ... or your father! It looks like you are two of a kind.'

'But ...?'

'Patrick Hagen,' she said. 'How could you?'

She went out of the room, and up the stairs.

'Mum,' I shouted. 'Mum!'

Her bedroom door slammed.

I went after her, up the stairs, and then I was down on my knees, banging and banging at her old door.

Then I was sitting on the stairs, and Gerry came and brought me down again.

'Leave go of me,' I said. 'I don't want you to touch me!'

She shrugged, and sat down.

I sat down too.

It was like a tea-party, only it wasn't. No tea, for one thing but we were having a party, all right!

The Belly stirred uncomfortably. He's an old man, as fat as three. There he was, with his hurley stick, lined up to act as our Home Guard, against all-comers.

'I'm very sorry you got mixed up in all this, Mr Kelly,' I said. 'I think you should go home now, if you don't mind, because I have things to say to my Mum and my sister.'

He didn't budge.

'I haven't done anything, and I don't understand all this, so help me God!' I burst out.

'I'll make a cup of tea,' Gerry said, and she went into the kitchen.

'That's a bloody irrelevant thing to do!' I shouted.

Old Belly spoke.

'You're in a bad mess, daughter,' he said. It is a country way of speaking, that, calling people daughter. I used to think it was funny when I first heard him.

'Yes, well, how do I get out of it?' I said.

'Take the boat,' he said, meaning get-on-your-bike.

'That's what I was going to do anyway,' I said. 'So thanks for nothing!' I was really mad. Nobody seemed to see it my way. They were all just sitting there saying I should let myself be driven out, when I hadn't done a thing to deserve it.

115

Sex and sin ... a real Irish brew. Even the bloody revolutionaries switched onto that combination automatically. My Dad went off with a woman and gave her her Daisy, and suddenly turning away the Collection Box for Prisoners' Dependants became a sign of something worse, and I was his daughter and didn't mind telling them what I thought, so I must be in it with the cops, and if I was like him one way I was like him another and must be bed-hopping with Patrick!

Why not *her*? Why not Gerry? She was his daughter too ... but then she'd kept her head down, stayed at the Convent School .. not thrown it all back in the face of the nuns and taken up with Protestant boyfriends and staged yelling matches in Con's house with somebody who later got a bullet put in him.

They probably didn't care whether the things they said about me were true or not, so long as they got their sacrifice. It's a sacrificial society ... blood for the Cause. If sending the word out on me, that I was talking to the cops and sleeping round, that I was raping Santa Claus and giving good Catholics Aids ... all that, whatever came into their heads ... if that meant that I had to get out ... well, it demonstrated to everybody else that you can't break the rules, didn't it? And that was just what they needed ... Pearce and his friend dead, Con arrested ... *but we got the one that did it.*

'JESUS CHRIST!' Gerry said, in the kitchen, and she came flying back out of it.

'There's someone in our ditch!' she said.

Old Belly was up out of his chair like a shot, with the hurley stick in his hands.

He went over to the light, and switched it off.

I went cold.

116

'Oh, Frankie!' Gerry said, crouching down beside me. We were behind the sofa, in case something came in through the back window.

Our kitchen lets out of our sitting-room. If anything came through the back window, the partition would probably save us ... depending what it was ... if it were bullets, you have no hope, but you're all right with stones and bottles. It was the stones-and-bottles brigade we were up against, probably, not the gunmen.

'Help!' Gerry said.

'Shut up,' I said.

We stayed put, praying.

Then there was a scuffling sound in the back yard, and the next moment someone tapped on the glass.

'Get away out of that, you bastard!' old Belly roared in the kitchen. He might be an old man, but he was like a man mountain when he moved.

Crash! Out through the back door, flailing with his hurley stick, and all the bins went over.

We dashed for the kitchen, and then Belly threw somebody in through the door .. our attacker. Only it wasn't an attacker. It was my Dad.

'Holy Jesus, Belly!' he said.

'You were in the yard, Joe ...' old Belly said.

'What are you doing here?' I said.

'You wanted me to come, so I came, Frankie,' he said.

Gerry never said a word. She went out of the room, and sat down in the armchair in the front.

'You're none too soon, Joe,' old Belly said.

'There's a crowd gathered,' my Dad said. 'Down the street. I came in the back way to avoid them.'

'We'll sort it out, the pair of us,' old Belly said.

'Sort *what* out?' my Dad said.

'You don't even bloody know!' I shouted at him.

Then the thing came through the window.

There was a big WHOOOSH! and the whole room was up and burning around us, and I was burning too, and going backward towards the door and my Dad caught me and then I was down on the floor and he was rolling on me and trying to beat out the flames and I could hear Gerry shrieking and my Dad was on fire and I was too and he got me up and we kind of bashed our way through the back out to the yard and that is the last bit I remember.

Chapter 15

The next bit I remember is being in the hospital. They must have had me sedated, or something, because the memory is only there in flashes.

I was in a bed up at the end of something like a corridor, only it can't have been a corridor, but it wasn't a ward.

They kept coming in to stop me shouting, and I kept asking them was Gerry all right, and was my Mum all right, and they kept saying yes-dear-everybody-is-all-right, and I was just to lie, but I couldn't lie still, and I didn't believe them.

They must have shot something stiffer into me, because the thing I remember after the room that *wasn't* a room, was a room, closed off from the others, and I was lying in it in the bed and there was a droning noise coming out of me and I knew I was being a nuisance and I knew I was in hospital and I knew I was keeping everybody up ... because I knew it was night, as well, that time, the time of the droning because it was dark but I couldn't stop the noise, it kept coming out of me. It wasn't a drone, really, just a low *aaaaaaaaaaaaaa* that kept coming out of me and wouldn't stop. It went on and on and on and on and on and then they must have come in and done something to me because the next thing I remember was another morning ... it was probably the second or third morning after ... and I was all right.

I was warm and cumfy, but I couldn't move. Some sort of straps on the bed. And there was something wrong with my eyes, and my face.

It was bruises and stitches, but I didn't know it. I was lucky it wasn't burns. The burns were on other bits of me.

I was all stiff and it hurt, in the middle of the sleepy cumfyness I knew that it hurt.

Then a nurse came. She wasn't a nurse I knew before, just somebody who was nice. She said was I awake, and I said I was, or I tried to say I was, but it didn't come out right, because my lips were fat and swollen.

'Just you lie there now, and don't fret a bit,' she said, cheerfully.

My Mum came.

She had her hat on, and Gerry was with her, only they wouldn't let Gerry talk to me. They just let her stand at the foot of my bed and make faces.

My Mum was crying.

'Can you hear me?' she kept saying.

And then she went away.

There was nothing wrong with my hearing, anyway. I could *hear* her, but there was nothing in me to respond with and I couldn't work out how one time I could get through to the nurse and the next time I couldn't speak to my Mum, but it must have been the effect of the painkillers and stuff.

My Dad didn't come at all, that day.

He came later, when I was able to sit up, only I wasn't right yet. I couldn't think two things connected. It must have been whatever the doctors put into me.

'What's happened to me?' I asked him.

'You're my own girl,' he said.

Well, maybe I was, but that wasn't much help. I tried to tell him that, but all that came out was 'What's happened to me?' He couldn't tell me, or maybe they wouldn't let him say, that seems more likely ... I felt like going to sleep instead of trying to talk to him, and I was asleep before he managed to say anything sensible.

I don't know when it was that they told me. I can't remember. I can't remember much at all about that time, only people coming that I wanted to tell me things, who couldn't, or wouldn't, or maybe it was that they were telling me, but I couldn't take it in. My head was all messed up inside, but I didn't know it.

It was only later on that I found out, and now I don't know what was true, because I have no real memory now of what happened ... only the memory of what I told people had happened ... and what I told them was that the thing came through the window and I sort of caught it ... only it wasn't there to catch, because it had shattered on the way through the window and when it hit me it was already going WHOOOSH, so I was right there in the middle of the glass and the splinters and the flame and the blazing petrol. I was doused in it and blasted back, and that's when my Dad got me and rolled me about the floor and got the fire out.

Then they got me out the back of the house, and they got me to hospital, but I don't know anything about that, because I wasn't there, but sometimes I think I can remember being in the ambulance, because the bumps hurt going down the road, only I don't know if I do remember, because it is all a mess and a muddle in my brain.

Well, the petrol burned me, and the glass cut me. I could have lost both eyes, but I didn't. The lids were sliced up, but not the eyeballs. There was a cut around the side of my head that they thought came from the window glass. It could have severed my head, but it didn't. There were wee cuts all over me, in the middle of the burns.

The burns weren't bad at all, when you think what they might have been. My Dad must have been quick. They're worst around my middle, where the marks will still be when they put me in my box, but I'll learn to live with that, I suppose.

And that's about it.

When the time came Mrs Walsh and my Dad drove me to the plane, and I went to Heathrow and out on the Tube to my Auntie Agnes, at the far end of the District Line.

That's where I am. Braintree, in Essex.

My Mum and Gerry moved. The Housing Executive put them on the Priority List. They are out at Portallen in a bungalow and my Mum says they'll leave if there is any trouble, but they don't think there will be, because I was the one they were after, not anybody else.

My Mum and Dad aren't talking. Why would they be? My Dad is still with Mrs Evans, helping look after the baby, Daisy.

I got a job.

It isn't much of a job. I'm house and baby minder for a woman. She comes from Enniskillen, and me and my disasters give her something to talk about at her dinner parties.

It is all flat here, and there are no mountains, but I'm doing ordinary things, the things I'd almost forgotten you could, and nobody knows who I am or what I am except my Auntie, and she turns out to be as mad as me anyway.

I've my *own* life to lead, and I'm getting on with it. Nobody's going to know what I'm about, and nobody's going to lay down what I should or shouldn't think, or should or shouldn't be.

It is funny, being free.

It takes a bit of getting used to.